ADVANCED REVIEWS

KIRKUS REVIEW

A compelling depiction of grief's impact that effectively makes use of its Icelandic backdrop.

The narrative moves at a well-paced clip to introduce its main characters and conversation and conflict with one another.

READERS VIEWS

Once in a while, we stumble upon a book that not only offers escapist entertainment, but also presents impressive takeaways to carry along during different seasons of life.

One such book is "His Final Answer", a vividly layered story packed with emotional truths.

Here co-authors Christopher White and Jennifer Curran embrace all the brittle fragments of grief and sorrow, hope and love.

A good book has the ability to elicit a change in us, this text unarguably does that.

(Lily Andrews / 5 Star review)

READERS FAVORITE

The portrayal of Daniel Pallson's profound emptiness, despite his wealth, struck a poignant chord. This was achieved with detailed close narration that allows readers into his psyche, but never spoon feeds the audience too much…

the return to Iceland was gorgeously penned with a strong shift of mood that was a powerful backdrop for Daniels confrontation with past life he had shut out.

(K.C. Finn /5 Stars out of 5)

His Final Answer is an engrossing character-driven about loss, grief and redemption. Recommended to readers of character driven tales.

(Pikasho Deka /5 Stars out of 5)

The authors' ability to depict Daniel's transformation from a hardened businessman to a man seeking forgiveness and reconciliation is particularly noteworthy. Highly recommended to those who appreciate emotionally rich stories that offer hope and a deeply satisfying resolution.

(Manik Chaturmutha /5 Stars out of 5)

I loved the contrast White and Curran created between Daniel's earthly and spiritual life. I enjoyed this book with its lovely characters, the beautiful portrayal of this unimaginable grief, and how one can live a peaceful life with acceptance and gratitude despite it.

(Jennie More /5 stars out of 5)

His Final Answer is a thought-provoking novel by Christopher D. White and Jennifer Curran. The dialogue between the characters is easy to follow. This unique drama offers profound personal loss and reconciliation lessons inviting readers to reflect on their experiences and relationships. (Essian Asian/ 5 Stars out of 5)

US REVIEW OF BOOKS

Christopher White has teamed up Jennifer Curran to create a mesmeric family drama that grapples with unresolved trauma and the renewal of faith.

The novel is a well-paced read that follows the trajectory of multiple characters' lives and the choices they make. Curran writes that this project was deeply personal due to the loss of her 23 year old sister to senseless tragedy.

ON LINE BOOK CLUB

People grieve differently. His Final Answer is a beautiful and touching story of Daniel Pallson, who lost his only son.

To find out how the story unfolds, grab a copy of His Final Answer…the plot itself is well developed, and the characters easy to love and understand because each one had their distinct personalities.

DAN BROWN ACADEMY

(pro beta readers)

A masterful collaboration by White and Curran offering readers an emotional journey through the shattered world of Big Deal Dan Pallson.

(George S.)

A gripping page turner that demands to be read in one sitting, leaving readers on the edge until the final revelation.

(Thomas L.)

White and Curran create a literary symphony of emotions, each chapter resonating with the harmonies of love, loss, and redemption.

(Martin K.)

A narrative that strikes a chord in the readers heart, blending the melodies of pain and healing in a beautiful literary composition.

(David B.)

Curran's poetic sensibility shines through in "His Final Answer". Adding a lyrical layer to the narrative that elevates it to literary excellence.

(Lauren M.)

The raw emotions portrayed in "His Final Answer" create an immersive reading experience, inviting readers to connect with the characters on a profound level.

(Rose E.)

ALSO AVAILABLE NOW
SPECIAL ILLUSTRATED PAPERBACK EDITION

20+ FULL-COLOR PAGE ILLUSTRATIONS THROUGHOUT THE BOOK

A GREAT GIFT
PURCHASE NOW!
HISFINALANSWER.COM

HISFINALANSWER.COM

HIS
FINAL
ANSWER

CHRISTOPHER D. WHITE

JENNIFER CURRAN

His Final Answer

Copyright © 2024 by Christopher D. White. All rights reserved.

No part of this book may be used or reproduced in any manner whatsoever without written permission, except in the case of brief quotations embodied in critical articles and reviews. For more information, e-mail all inquiries to info@mindstirmedia.com.

MINDSTIR MEDIA

Published by MindStir Media, LLC
45 Lafayette Rd | Suite 181 | North Hampton, NH 03862 | USA
1.800.767.0531 | www.mindstirmedia.com
Printed in the United States of America.
ISBN-13: 978-1-963844-06-1

DEDICATION
BY JENNIFER CURRAN

CHRIS AND I have known each other for years, and I knew he was coming off his latest excellent film, High Expectations. I ran into him and asked him if he knew what his next project would be.

A few years ago, he told me he had yet another idea of doing something special related to multiple friends of his who experienced what many say is the worst tragedy in the world. Those who lost a child (mostly in their teens or early twenties) in different ways. One night, a best friend of Chris's, who was also a very prominent American entrepreneur, opened up after years and admitted that when people thought he was doing better after years of losing his son, he still had never gone one day without grieving beyond belief, and the angst never seemed to even take a pause, even decades later. Chris had no idea, as his friend seemed to be able to carry on more and more as the years went on. He told Chris it was nothing more than a facade he had learned to portray. Chris never had a child, but that statement from one of his best friends shook him unlike anything else.

I told Chris how I lost my best friend, who was my older sister, in a tragedy when she was only twenty-three. She had the flu at her apartment, fell, and hit her head with no roommates around. As they were out for New Years Eve.

I spoke for a few hours about how it changed my life and how I had to watch my poor parents suffer as they continued to raise the other nine of us with little time or ability to properly grieve. The loss does affect so many for the rest of their lives. Honestly, some more than others. But still, how do those who actually suffered such a tragedy ever find a way to go on? Then there's all the collateral damage to marriages, self-guilt, pessimism, faith, and so much more.

Chris said this fascinated him, and he wanted to tell a fictitious story based around these real sufferers, first as a novel and then as his next film to direct and produce off this book. He had heard I was a writer, former playwright, actress and asked me if I was interested in discussing co-writing the novel, especially after hearing about my own experience with my beloved sister. Upon our first meeting, we knew we were meant to write this novel together. We are very proud of this work.

'I SELDOM END UP WHERE I WANTED TO GO, BUT ALMOST ALWAYS END UP WHERE I NEED TO BE.'

—Douglas Adams

CONTENTS

About the Authors ▶ **xix**

Preface ▶ **xxiii**

chapter 1
Brothers in Arms ▶ **1**

chapter 2
Matters of the Heart ▶ **11**

chapter 3
Perceptions and Privilege ▶ **21**

chapter 4
Sun Spots on the Farm ▶ **31**

chapter 5
New Faces, Old Places ▶ **41**

chapter 6
The Interview ▶ **49**

CHAPTER 7
Coming Back Home ▸ **59**

CHAPTER 8
Picture of the Past ▸ **67**

CHAPTER 9
Looking for What Is Lost ▸ **73**

CHAPTER 10
Catch and Release ▸ **81**

CHAPTER 11
The Current of Memories ▸ **89**

CHAPTER 12
The Dream ▸ **96**

CHAPTER 13
The Surprise Visit ▸ **105**

CHAPTER 14
The Biggest Deal ▸ **114**

CHAPTER 15
Reality of Suffering ▸ **128**

CHAPTER 16
One Last Time ▸ **141**

CHAPTER 17
Screaming and Shouting ▸ **148**

CHAPTER 18
The Best Bet ▶ **154**

CHAPTER 19
Last Call ▶ **160**

CHAPTER 20
The Biggest Deal of All ▶ **165**

ABOUT THE AUTHORS

JENNIFER CURRAN

Jennifer Curran was born and raised in the state of Vermont in the small, great town of Stamford with a population of only 800. A true American, next-door-type girl, Jennifer not only was awarded the school patriot award in high school but also excelled in basketball, softball, and skiing, as her father was in charge of the Ski School at the nearby Dutch Ski Hill.

Jennifer attended Boston University on an English scholarship, which was interrupted by being discovered walking down a street in New York at the age of nineteen and offered a contract with the world-renowned Elite Modeling Agency. Within weeks, she was off to Australia to film a Japanese beer commercial then over to Paris and the world for the next ten years to model.

She returned to the US (New York City), where she started at an off-Broadway theater group out of the Chelsea Hotel. From there, she went to California to pursue her acting and writing dreams. An avid poet and short story writer, she's a certified member of the renowned Amherst

Writers and Artists organization. This is Jennifer's first novel co-written with Mr. White.

CHRISTOPHER D. WHITE

A product of the Midwest, born and raised in the Chicagoland area of neighboring northwest Indiana. Like most of the boys growing up there in the sixties, his main interests were all sports and all Chicago teams. (Christopher also realized a dream of receiving a genuine Chicago Cubs 2016 World Series ring as part owner of the team during that time.) Christopher graduated from Indiana University in 1981 with a business degree, worked for a major Wall Street firm as a stockbroker located in the Los Angeles area, and performed at area amateur comedy clubs at night, telling jokes he had been writing for years. He decided then he must pursue his creative endeavors, including filmmaking, of which he had no experience. He took a film writing class at UCLA at night, which changed his life in that direction. He wrote one script from that class and submitted it as part of an application to the prestigious and highly competitive American Film Institute, with no previous filmmaking experience whatsoever.

Incredibly, the script was so well received that Christopher was accepted against all odds as a producing fellow. After surviving ten years as a struggling writer, mostly taking odd jobs, including as a movie extra and even driving a cab, Christopher got his first film, which he wrote and produced in 2002, called Missing Brendan, starring Ed Asner and giving a very young Adam Brody his first dramatic film role. Christopher also authored a very well-received dedication book about the WWII generation written in the year 2000. He also followed this up with other known film and TV projects, including as a producer on the Netflix series Vahalia Murders.

He directed and produced a few documentaries, including directing, writing, and producing the film High Expectations in 2023, starring Kelsey Grammer and giving singer Ally Brooke her dream of starring in her first movie. There are plans to make this novel, His Final Answer, a film to be made mostly in Iceland and Boston, with Mr. White directing, writing, and producing.

PREFACE
BY CHRISTOPHER D. WHITE

A FEW DECADES ago, I saw a television interview with one of my favorite actors, who I knew was suffering from a major illness and didn't have long to live. I knew he had lost a child to a tragedy about twenty years ago, but I was shocked at what he said that day. He said he never spent one day without feeling devastated about his twenty-three-year-old son, and with tears he said he wanted to apologize to those he shut out for so long because of his incomplete grief. He had endless self-guilt, anger, and doubt about the whole world after being a well-known optimist his entire life. I thought how sad that was. For some reason, that stuck with me enough to write about this years later, as I experienced some of my best friends having to go through the same loss of losing a child. I wondered how possibly they could get through it. This compelled me to write a story about it. Shortly thereafter, I met with Jennifer Curran to work on the novel with me.

This book was written for that actor and all others who have had to experience such an unimaginably painful event. Actually, I think this novel can easily apply to many cases of grief for loved ones who have lost others, whether it be family or others. This book explains how never getting better at any grief can rival the negative effects of the actual tragedy of years ago. I think the protagonist covers what we, the writers, mean with regard to this and much more.

There are other main characters who add so much to this story. We know writing this book is as true as it gets, as it has caused a impact in both our (co-writers) lives for writing it.

CHAPTER 1
BROTHERS IN ARMS

It was a beautiful, sunny day. The sharp blue sky stood out in contrast with the floating cumulus clouds. Underneath was a luscious, deep-green valley, a moving, clear river, either side of it enveloped by majestic snow-capped mountains brimming with life.

Two men stood in the water, one near the rocky shore, the other in the depths, both outfitted in well-worn chest waders, both smoothly working the lines. One would reel in another salmon, brown trout, or arctic char, unhook it, store it in the basket, and then re-bait their hooks to throw back in. A few times, one would catch a smaller fish, unhook it, and release it. The only disturbances of the calm being the soul-soothing whirl of the lines being sent and the splashing of the occasional catch.

At the top of the hill, there was a road that led down to the valley below to a large gate, closing off the traffic to the public. Just outside the gate, a large procession of protesters had gathered, impatience showing on their faces, awaiting the long overdue court decision regarding Salmon Valley, the proposed luxury hotel and fishing resort.

Inside the resort, Daniel Pallson stood at a podium. He was sixty-seven years old and was considered one of the wealthiest men in the world. Wearing a flawlessly tailored Italian blue suit, Daniel had the kind of charm and charisma that would engulf any room he walked into. A person could tell there was something special about him with just a glance, and he was known for his no-nonsense attitude. He exuded power, was undeniably handsome, and, at 6'3" stood taller than most around him. He had hard-earned lines on his face and a full but rather gray, clean-cut beard.

Many thought a man's eyes told the most about him, but with Daniel always wearing smokey tinted glasses this was difficult to do. Was this intentional not to show too much of what lied behind those eyes? Others thought a man's shoes told the most about him. As impeccably as Daniel was dressed today, his Prada boots looked a bit worn and certainly not spotless. Did this really show anything about him, or did he just wear that pair knowing he was going to a muddy river for the ceremony?

Standing next to Daniel was fifty-six-year-old Council Member Karlsson, Major Magnusson from the next town, and Stephan, a forty-seven-year-old all-rounder who was Daniel's point person in Iceland and was overseeing the Salmon River project. He took care of anything Daniel needed immediately whenever asked and was considered his right-hand man by the locals. He was also a man who carried himself with power.

In attendance were politicians, the minister of industry, as well as a variety of well-wishing influential VIPs. It was undoubtedly a big moment for Iceland. As Daniel walked around the room, shaking hands and exchanging smiles, a large number of attendees were transfixed by the masterful rendering of the resort, which was placed on an easel near the microphone and projected on the wall behind a podium fitted with microphones.

Outside the resort, however, was an entirely different feeling and scene. Dozens of protesters walked up and down the gateway, holding signs written in Icelandic that, translated into English, read, "DON'T RUIN OUR LAND" and "ICELAND IS NOT FOR SALE." The crowd was beginning to grow restless as the news teams made their presence known by beginning their live telecast of the event. Inside the newsroom, Ted Witt addressed all those tuned in.

"We have breaking news regarding the long-standing, high-profile resort development in Iceland. The controversy continues to swirl around billionaire Daniel Pallson, also known in world business circles as Big Deal Dan." As he spoke, stunning images of the mural, the surrounding land, and the river were being televised across the world.

"After years of legal battle, Daniel Pallson is finally going to build the hotel and fishing resort he promised would be the greatest in the world. It was signed off by the prime minister of Iceland as well as the minister of Industry. It seems Iceland's own prodigal son has returned. Let's go to Susan Hernandez, who is present at the scene in Iceland," said Ted as the screen switched over to Susan.

"Thank you, Ted. This situation has become big news here in Iceland, a small but determined country famously forged from fire and ice. These people here today, many of whom are descendants of the Vikings, the mighty clan that centuries ago somehow survived in this unforgiving land. Also known as part of Icelands lore is the Irish Monks who had sailed to this land in search of solitude but left after the mostly godless Pagan Nordic settlers arrived.

"It should never be forgotten that Iceland's very existence was in jeopardy during WWII, as Adolph Hitler was known to be considering an invasion. German submarines actually destroyed some ships in the local harbors. Iceland today still faces serious threats from lurching volcanoes to the reason why we here today. There has been an ongoing hot debate on both sides, mostly from Icelanders who feel foreigners are stealing their country, which is somewhat strange since Daniel was born in Iceland.

"And here's another twist. With me is Pastor Jon Pallson, Daniel's younger brother, who has become the most fervent opponent and the leading protestor against his brother's development." Susan turned to Jon, a fit man in his early sixties. He was a known advocate for growing environmental issues in Iceland and a forerunner in spreading awareness about clean energy and conservation in a changing world. His long, gray hair was combed back into a neat bun, and his beard was meticulously groomed.

"Pastor, can I get your feelings about this decision by your own government about this planned development on your family estate, which your own brother won in another legal battle five years ago?" Susan asked him, pointing her hand-held microphone in his direction, waiting for an answer.

"I am obviously disappointed. As you know, I'm a big opponent of this project and feel that way about anything potentially harmful to the environment," he stated with calm assurance. "I pray that we all take the environment seriously, as we are to leave this beautiful land to the next generations."

"Tell me, Jon, why are you so against your brother?" Susan persisted, but Jon remained collected and composed despite the repetitiveness of the question. Even though it was a common point of conversation due to how prominent a figure his brother was, the question regarding his own family still made him feel uncomfortable. On the surface, however, there was not a single crack in his façade.

"I have nothing against my brother, but we differ greatly on this issue," he told her, looking her in the eye instead of the camera. Susan ignored the hint and continued with her line of questioning.

"So is it true that you haven't spoken since the previous litigation years ago over the estate?"

"That is between my brother and I, and I consider that a private matter," he responded firmly, trying to keep the edge of annoyance out of his tone.

"But you won't deny it?" Susan continued.

"Family matters have nothing to do with this, Susan. This is about our country, nothing more."

"Thank you. The coalition will release a statement at the end of the day," Jon answered, walking off and rejoining the crowd, realizing that Susan's agenda was solely on stirring up controversy and ratings. He turned away, and immediately Susan turned her attention to Daniel and his entourage, who had just made their appearance.

"It looks like Daniel Pallson is coming to address the crowd," Susan announced to the camera as all eyes shifted toward Daniel. It was Karlsson though who stepped up to the outer podium and was met with boos from the crowd. Two policemen from the next town were present, watching over the crowd, gauging their unrest.

"This is by far the best thing that has happened in the East Fjords for years," he said into the mic, which elicited even more jeers and boos from the protestors. "We are about to open this beautiful resort for business. Wild salmon and other varieties of native species for those sportsmen and women from around the world who love the best fishing in the world. We welcome all of you and your families to enjoy the great activities Iceland has to offer. I want to introduce to you the man who made all this possible. Please, welcome a native son of Iceland, Daniel Pallson," Karlsson concluded as he stepped away from the microphone, making room for Daniel to walk up. Scattered applause came only from his supporters and the VIPs in attendance.

"Thank you, Councilman Karlsson. It's always good to be back home!" Daniel said warmly to the crowd with a smile on his face.

Someone in the crowd loudly called out, "Give us a break. You're not home, and you are not Icelandic anymore. It's all about money!" Cheers of agreement came from the other protesters. Daniel carried on without missing a beat.

"I know that a lot of people here do not agree with me, but you will see in time that what we are doing here is conserving the great Icelandic fish. There is no equal to our wild salmon in the world! Our venture will bring prosperity and job opportunities to the community. Trust me, this development will be a turning point for this land and its people," Daniel emphasized.

The jeers from the crowd got louder at this statement, and it became even harder to hear what Daniel had to say. He had to raise his voice. "Which is what we all want! I want to thank all the supporters, including the Icelandic government, Major Magnusson, and Councilman Karlsson. This has been a long, arduous process for approval but will be worth it—"

He was cut off by an egg that went sailing through the air and landed square on Karlsson's face. Right on cue, a barrage of tomatoes and eggs were thrown toward Daniel and the podium. Jon could be seen trying to move through the crowd to get to his brother. He was not expecting the crowd to get rowdy, but by now the people had formed a tight barricade, and reaching Daniel was impossible. Daniel, Councilman Karlsson, and Major Magnusson were immediately escorted inside the side room of the resort as the protesters continued throwing eggs and tomatoes in their direction.

Once they were inside the room, Daniel looked around at them and chuckled, "That went well."

"It is just another day for us in the line of fire. But well worth it," Karlsson said, wiping the remnants of the egg yolk off his face.

"In time, the protests will subside. We are used to facing protestors and critics. You see, change isn't easily accepted, but it is inevitable. Thank you both for the assist though," Daniel told them in earnest.

"Let's see how it unfolds. Unfortunately, the quiet days seem to be getting fewer and farther apart. No one can agree on anything anymore," commented Mugnusson as he handed Karlsson another tissue.

"That doesn't surprise me. That's the same way my stockholder meetings seem to be going too," replied Daniel wryly as they all laughed. There was a table with a thermos of coffee kept at the side of the room, and he walked over to make himself a mug, no sugar, just black. He peered out the window and saw Susan still reporting on the scene and the crowd of protestors dispersing.

"As you witnessed just now, the protesters took to violence, and the police have arrested a few. No injuries have been reported, but the debate is certainly heating up. Ted, back to you," Susan said, signing off and taking out her earpiece as the cameraman started packing up the gear.

Jon surveyed the scene as the crowd was still chanting slogans, but the news vans were now wrapping up. He looked at the beautiful landscape in front of him and sighed. Change was coming. He wanted to speak to his brother. It had been quite a while since the two had talked. And given what had just happened and the kind of reaction Daniel had gotten from the crowd, Jon wanted to reach out. He called Daniel, who cut the call as soon as he saw his name pop up on the screen.

Daniel frowned as he cut Jon's call. He didn't have time for this. He walked back to join the men, leaning over to Stephan before whispering for him to get the helicopter ready. As Stephan sprang into action, Daniel cleared his throat. "Now, gentleman, let's leave this godforsaken crowd and get back to my plane. We have all earned a few sips from that nectar of the Gods I talked about."

"I was hoping you would bring that up." Karlsson grinned as Mugnusson laughed in agreement. Daniel said his goodbyes to the supporters before leading the way to the helicopter.

As they entered the open air, several feet away from where the chopper had started its blades, someone yelled out, "Danny!" The men turned to see Jon briskly walking toward where they were.

"Carry on. I'll be right there," Daniel called out to the men as he stood waiting for Jon. "What is it?" he asked when Jon finally caught up.

"Were you planning on taking off without speaking to me?" Jon questioned.

"What is there to talk about?" a stone-faced Daniel asked, unwilling to meet his brother's eye.

"Come on, Danny, it's me. We have always been able to talk."

"Well, you should've thought of that before you took me to court," Daniel replied coldly, turning to walk away, but Jon grabbed him by the shoulder and spun him back around.

"You left me no choice!" argued Jon, trying desperately to make Daniel see the sense in his words.

"I know we have had our differences in the past, but this was a new low!"

"Again, dragging the past into this. I just want people to be able to enjoy the valley and the beach. Just like our parents wanted," he said softer than he meant to.

"Don't bring them into this. They would be ashamed of you!" Daniel yelled, having lost control of his composure over the mention of his parents.

"Really! Look who's talking! And this isn't personal anymore. It's about what you are doing with the valley," Jon explained emphatically, even though it was clear his words were just making Daniel angrier.

"You got the ranch. Isn't that what you always wanted?" Daniel asked in a raised voice, anger in his eyes, the color flushing his face.

"Is that it? Me getting the ranch?" asked Jon, exasperated.

"You were always the favorite!" Daniel screamed, reaching his limit. He breathed deeply and smoothed his hair back.

"You never change. It is always about business first," said Jon.

Daniel shot his brother a final look and made his way to the helicopter. Jon watched him walk away, equal parts frustrated and helpless. Getting through to Daniel, even after all these years, was still near impossible. Age had done nothing to soften up the man.

CHAPTER 2
MATTERS OF THE HEART

THE HELICOPTER LANDED on the helipad, and the men got out and began walking toward the private jet, its door already open with the ladder extended.

Daniel liked opulence; he had worked hard for it and was proud of how far he had come in life. And since time was a luxury Daniel could ill afford, he was glad to have made such an investment in luxury and comfort. This new top model G6 business jet was another in a long line of Gulfstreams he owned and used to travel across the world for over thirty years.

"Ready for a taste of the best thirty-year-old whiskey you will ever have?" Daniel called out with a grin.

"Single, not blended. If it's good enough for Daniel Pallson, it's good enough for me," replied Karlsson, eager to get on the plane.

"Amen to that!" added Stefan, who was one step behind them, his briefcase swinging away as he walked.

"It was personally hand-delivered to me last week by the prime minister of Scotland!" announced Daniel as the men cheered in excitement. As they walked, Daniel suddenly stopped in his tracks and kneeled. His one hand was propping him up while the other clutched at his chest. He felt a searing pain starting from his chest and traveling to his arm and jaw. It felt as if a giant boulder was being placed on his heart.

Seeing Daniel stagger and clutch his heart, Magnusson swooped down and helped support him while Karlsson looked on with concern.

"Are you okay?" Magnusson asked, alarmed.

"It's my heart," Daniel managed to sputter out as he gasped for air. "I can't breathe."

His eyes began to bulge as his breathing seemed to constrict even further. The man was sweating profusely, yet his skin took on a slightly blue tinge, and Magnusson realized he needed to act quickly. In a flash, he removed Daniel's tie and unbuttoned his top buttons, allowing him to breathe more freely. He looked in the direction of the helicopter and yelled out, "Get him toward the chopper, fast. We need to take him to the nearest hospital!"

Stefan quickly made a call on his phone, and the blades of the helicopter started again in full throttle as Karlsson and Magnusson quickly lifted and carried Daniel over to the helicopter.

* * *

Inside an office building sat Pastor Jon Pallson at a press conference with the environmental coalition. He was sitting next to Kristinn Thordarson, the speaker who ran the coalition, listening intently to what she had to say.

"It is obvious to all of us that Daniel will not stop here. He will continue building on the land. He might even try to force a casino onto the land. After all, that is what he is known for," Thompson said into the microphone, and instantly a reporter's hand shot up in response.

"But he can't build a casino in Iceland. It's against the law."

"I would not put anything past this man," Thompson told the reporter with a grimace on her face. At that moment, Pastor Jon's phone vibrated, and he looked down at the screen, which showed a text message from Stephan. ***Please call me as soon as you read this! Urgent!***

Jon got up from his seat and went outside the conference hall to call him.

"Yes, Stefan, what is it?" Jon inquired.

"Daniel has gone into cardiac arrest. We've just brought him to the hospital. They are asking for the next of kin," Stefan explained.

"Oh no! Which hospital? I'll be there." Jon hurriedly cut the call and then rushed back in to pick up his belongings, too anxious to make eye contact with a concerned Thompson as he left.

He reached the hospital shortly after that and ran down the hall to the nurse's station.

"I am looking for Daniel Pallson," he told the nurse behind the counter, an elderly lady with a stern look about her. "How is he?" he asked, a little out of breath.

"May I ask your relation to him? Sorry, but we are not allowed to disclose information about our patients to the public," she told him, peering up from her black-rimmed glasses.

"That's fine. I'm his brother, Jon Pallson," he said, quickly taking his ID card out of his wallet and showing it to her. She looked at it, nodded, and handed it back to him.

"He's in the intensive care unit. The doctor would like to speak with you. Please wait here," she said, gesturing to the nearly full seats in the hall. Jon looked out at the sea of people from all walks of life, some with more severe grievances than others, and took a seat near the corner of the room. He bowed his head and prayed; it never failed to help calm his nerves, which were all over the place. He prayed for his brother's health and didn't want to even envisage anything going wrong.

He was still trying to come to terms with Daniel being back, and now he was hospitalized due to heart failure. His brother had seemed so full of vigor and determination just a while ago. Jon pondered over how situations could change in the blink of an eye. Life truly was fleeting, and there was nothing anyone could do about it. That had been man's fate, and it shall last till the end of times.

A few minutes later, he lifted his head and spotted Magnusson and Karlsson, who made eye contact with him and nodded. He would have gone over and greeted them, but both parties knew they really didn't have much to say to one another and that maintaining the polite distance between was what both of them wanted. Jon dug his cell phone out of his pocket and sent a text message to his wife, Doris, informing her of Daniel's condition and that he was at the hospital with him.

Just as he pressed send, he saw a doctor walk into the hall and the nurse pointing to him. He got up and went over to the doctor.

"Hello, Jon, I am Dr. Einarsson. I am handling Daniel's case," he told him, giving Jon a firm handshake.

"Hello, Doctor. How is he doing? Is he alright?" Jon asked nervously, his eyes flitting over to Magnusson and Karlsson, who were looking over in his direction attentively.

"Better now since the emergency surgery. It was a lot of luck that the helicopter was there and got him to us so quickly," the Doctor told him, and a wave of relief washed over Jon.

"So he is okay then?"

"We can't say for sure until he wakes up, but it looks like that," the doctor informed Jon calmly as he put a reassuring hand on his shoulder.

"Can I go see him?" Jon asked. The doctor nodded and motioned for Jon to follow him.

The doctor led Jon toward a window. Lying on the bed, Daniel was hooked up to various machines and hospital equipment. He looked incredibly fragile in this state, as if he had folded into himself, a shell of what he was. The strong and charismatic man from earlier that day was gone.

Seeing him this way was disconcerting for Jon, who immediately rushed to his side and took his brother's hand in his own.

"Is he going to be fine? He doesn't look well at all," Jon asked, still looking at Daniel.

"It was cardiac arrest, but it appears that the surgery was successful. We managed to clear out the two main arteries to the heart. I think he will be alright, but we are not completely out of the woods yet," Dr. Einarsson assured him then took his leave as Jon made himself comfortable on the small sofa next to the hospital bed.

* * *

Halfway across the world, Doris Pallson was getting ready to go out for a fundraiser. She gave one last look in the full-length mirror. Even at the age of sixty-two, Doris had kept herself fit, preserving her natural beauty. The maroon blazer and flared pants emphasized her small waist and slender frame.

Satisfied with her appearance and coiffed hair, she picked up her vintage Chanel bag and headed out. On the way, her phone started ringing, and seeing Jon's number appearing on the screen made her pause.

It had been a while since she had spoken to her estranged husband's brother. Taking a deep breath, she picked up the call.

"Hello, Jon. It's been a while," she murmured.

"Yes, it has. Daniel's in the hospital. He had a heart attack and is in the ICU here in Reykjavik. I thought, despite everything, you should know," Jon spoke without preamble.

"Oh my God!" Doris gasped, not expecting to hear this. "How is he now?"

"The surgery was a success, but he's still not out of the woods," Jon told her.

They spoke a little bit more about Daniel's condition before saying goodbyes. The thought of Daniel almost dying filled Doris with dread. It had been years since she had laid eyes on her husband. Their separation hadn't been amicable. Years of unexpressed resentment and grief had led to the separation of their marriage.

Doris had to start all over again, and now she ran the largest children's hospital foundation in Boston. Just now, she had been on her way to a fundraiser that would help add a new wing to her hospital for children suffering from Leukemia.

However, now she knew she couldn't go, not in the state she was in. She sent a text then called her secretary to make excuses on her behalf and to also book the first available flight to Iceland.

She quickly changed into comfortable clothes then packed her overnight suitcase.

After reaching the airport, she sat in the massive and luxuriously decorated club for first-class travelers going from Boston Logan to the main airport in Reykjavik. There were only a handful of people waiting, with a lot more staff serving the few clients.

She decided to call her long-time friend and spiritual advisor, Reverend Adams, before boarding.

Adams saw Doris's name flash across the screen and quickly answered, "Hello, Doris."

"Where are you? Are you taking off tonight?" Doris asked her.

"Yes, I was able to move my schedule around. You already sent me the needed info, and I will call you when I get in," the reverend said.

"Okay, great. That sounds good. Bye," Doris said, clicking off the call and walking through to board her plane.

* * *

In an office in Boston, Mr. Simon, a man in his mid-fifties who was balding as well as a bit overweight, was sweating profusely despite the air conditioning being cranked to full blast. He was in charge of the meeting and was now relaying the news to the people present.

"There was a major blockage. We don't know the extent of it yet. He just came out of surgery," he told the two executives and lawyer Phil Wood, the only three other members present besides himself.

"Any idea how limited he is going to be?" snapped Phil, thoroughly agitated with the situation he had found himself in. He was a sharp-minded and calculative man.

"I honestly don't know. It's impossible to tell until he wakes up," Mr. Simon admitted in a squeaky, nervous voice.

"Is anyone going to Iceland?" one of the executives asked, his tone sounding even more strained than Phil's.

"Simon and I will go. We will be ready to leave shortly," Phil informed them as he stood up and smoothed his coat jacket.

"Do we need to make a statement?" the other executive asked him before he and Simon left the room.

"Let's hold off for now until we find out how he is. Best case is if he can do it himself, that will keep shareholders calm," Phil replied before leaving.

* * *

The next morning, Daniel had been taken out of intensive care and moved to a regular room, where Jon sat next to him on an uncomfortable lounge chair.

Doris entered the hospital room and walked straight to Daniel. She looked at the frail man in front of her and could feel her heart breaking. She put her hand next to his chin, almost afraid of touching him, as if he were a fragile thing and even touching might cause him harm. Then, after much deliberation, she touched him very tenderly, and it was obvious this was a woman who had known the man in the hospital bed for just over forty-five years and still cared for him very deeply.

Jon stirred and opened his eyes. Seeing Doris by Daniel's side, he got up, dusted off the crumbs from a packet of crackers he had gotten from the vending machine, and walked over to her.

"Glad you came, Doris. I'm so happy you're here," he told her gently as they both hugged each other.

"I came as fast as I could," she told him as they separated from one another. "How is he?" she asked, looking at Daniel's face as tears threatened to spill from her eyes.

"The doctors think it looks optimistic," Jon told her, looking over at Daniel, who was still sleeping after his surgery.

"Oh thank God," Doris said as Doctor Einarsson entered the room. He nodded at them before going to check up on Daniel's vitals.

"Hope you are doing okay. We ran some tests, and from the looks of it, all signs are good. We just need him to wake up," he informed them, looking over the chart attached to the clipboard at the end of Daniel's bed.

"Any clue when he will wake up?" Doris questioned, feeling much better since she had heard what the doctor had to say. He shrugged before answering, "Tomorrow morning at the earliest, I reckon. The next twelve hours are critical. We had to replace two valves of his heart. He is going to be pretty weak when he wakes up. Maybe you should go home and get some rest, as he won't be up at least till tomorrow morning," he suggested. "I believe the nurse has taken all of Jon's contact information. We will inform you right away in case anything changes before then."

Jon and Doris thanked the doctor, who then left the room.

"Let's come back in the morning, Doris. You must be tired from all the traveling," Jon said as Doris nodded in agreement, going over to Daniel one more time. She looked at him tenderly, her face reflective of concern, fear, and yearning. She sorely wanted to kiss him on the forehead but refrained. Instead, she took hold of his hand and gave it a slight squeeze.

Jon stood by the door, holding his briefcase and her bag as he waited for her. A wave of sadness hit him, seeing his brother and sister-in-law like this. Doris slowly turned, and they walked out of the room. They stopped at the nurses' station before leaving and requested to be called right away if Daniel woke up or if there was a change in his condition. All they could do now was wait.

CHAPTER 3
PERCEPTIONS AND PRIVILEGE

As Jon and Doris left the hospital, there was a slight drizzle, and an overall gloomy atmosphere had taken hold of the evening. They walked in silence side by side till they exited the hospital.

Doris stopped and turned her face upward toward the darkening sky, small droplets falling on her face.

"It feels weird being back," she said.

"Perhaps. But I believe you did the right thing by coming here," Jon added.

"Hmm… You won't mind dropping me off at the hotel, I hope?" asked Doris as she looked out onto the asphalt, which had turned dark gray due to the moisture.

"You don't need to go to the hotel. I have an apartment in the city that you are more than welcome to," offered Jon.

"My friend Reverend Adams is coming in a few days," she told him, not wanting to impose on the hospitality he was extending.

"You are family—I insist. And both of you should come to the farm. Anna would love to see you," Jon said, gesturing toward his car, which was parked nearby.

"Thank you, that would be nice. Maybe when Daniel has recovered," Doris mused as Jon opened the car door for her, and she got in. Now that she was here, all her anxieties were coming to the surface. It had been so long since Daniel and she had talked or faced each other. Coming to Iceland was a knee-jerk reaction to Daniel's illness. And seeing him lying in the hospital bed, hooked up to a monitor and IVs, truly shocked her.

"Why are you so silent? What are you thinking?" Jon asked, noticing she hadn't spoken in a while.

"Nothing, just tired, I guess," she answered.

"You need to keep up your strength. How about some food? I know the perfect place," Jon told her as he put the car in gear.

Doris nodded, and they began driving toward a quaint old restaurant in downtown Reykjavik. It was a place that had been around for a long time, with the interior emulating a typical Reykjavik apartment, albeit dated. It was truly an Icelandic establishment that had not changed in years, which added to its rustic charm.

"I can't believe this place is still open. I love the food here!" exclaimed Doris, sitting down and looking around as a waitress came up to them and handed them the menu.

"Remember back in the sixties when it was a watering hole for the intelligentsia?" Jon quipped.

"Of course, added so much mystique to the place. We're getting the carrot cake afterward. I still reminisce about it being the best I ever had, and that was a long time ago." Doris smiled.

They both ordered coffee and a meat soup to share, a common Icelandic dish comprising meat and vegetables in a thick stew. As they waited for their food, their attention was turned to the news report that was on a small television placed near the back of the restaurant.

"The hospital refuses to report on the condition of Iceland's native billionaire Daniel Pallson. He was reportedly admitted to the emergency room yesterday on his way to the Reykjavik airport on his way back to his adopted home in the US."

Jon asked a waitress who was walking by to turn it off, shaking his head at the probable implications the reports would have.

"These people are unbelievable," Jon said, shaking his head in disappointment.

Dorris added, "Don't give them a second thought. Tell me, how have you been, Jon?" She took a sip of her coffee before adding some more sugar to it.

"Been good, thank God. What about you?"

"Overall, fine. It's been pretty tough since I left him, but I couldn't go on like that anymore. All of it became too much," replied Doris, looking away and blinking back tears. It was hard for her to talk about her separation from Daniel, but she had always been close to Jon and realized this conversation was long overdue. After a pause, she asked him, "What did you think when you heard I was leaving him?"

"Honestly, I couldn't believe you stayed with him that long since he tuned everything out, including you," admitted Jon before finishing the remainder of his soup. The sound of soft jazz played in the background as one of the waitresses turned on an old recorder, humming along when it started to play.

"Thank you for saying that. You know, I never really liked the spotlight we found ourselves in once the business expanded to the scale it did." She sniffed.

"You were always supportive of him. And no one could foresee the business growing so fast," Jon said empathetically.

"Except maybe Daniel. Those early days in Connecticut were always my favorite. Simpler times," Doris said, smiling. Daniel had known right from the start how well the business would do, and he told Doris that on numerous occasions. The only thing he did not take into account was just how much he would lose along the way. "I remember how happy Thomas was as a boy. Always playing with his father," she said, a note of wistfulness in her tone.

"I remember when you wrote to me and told me when you thought you found peace after his passing. You still think that was the case then?" Jon asked her gently, reaching over and patting her hand. Doris quickly dabbed at a teardrop in her eyes as she made sure to gather herself.

"I have. But unfortunately I don't think Daniel has ever made peace with himself about what happened. He just grew angrier as time passed. It affected everything around him," she explained to him.

Jon then asked her something he had been meaning to for a long time, a question to which the answer mattered more than he cared to say. "And he never sought help? Or counseling?"

"No, and in the end I couldn't live with him anymore. He sought solace in his work, and I was left alone to deal with my grief. His work swallowed him up and our relationship with it."

"I can imagine. I've seen how driven he can be. Truth be told, grief needs to be processed, especially in a marriage. Partners need to deal with it together, and when that doesn't happen, things fall apart," Jon mused.

Doris nodded and focused on eating the carrot cake. Both of them understood that the conversation was over. Jon asked for the check while Doris went to the ladies' room to freshen up. It had been a long day, and she was at her limit both emotionally and physically.

After dropping off Doris and telling her to call him if she needed anything, Jon had driven home, looking forward to getting into bed. It had been a long day for him too.

"Hey, I'm glad he's out of danger. How are you holding up?" Jon's wife Anna embraced him. Jon looked weary and tired.

"I was scared. We could have lost him," Jon told her honestly, his voice hoarse.

* * *

The next morning, Jon picked Doris up from the apartment, and they headed to the hospital. They had only been sitting there for an hour reading when Daniel began to stir and mumble something.

"Where am I?" he said at last, blinking his eyes rapidly, unaware of his surroundings. Doris immediately sprung out of her seat and rushed to his side.

"Thank God you are okay," she said with a sigh of relief, her hand on her chest.

"What? What the hell are you doing here?" Daniel asked, his eyes fully open, looking around.

"You had heart surgery. And you are doing good," Doris told him. He still looked shocked and tried to make sounds of confusion when Jon stood up and came to his other side.

"Take it easy. You went into cardiac arrest at the airport while you were leaving. You're lucky to have survived," Jon told him. Daniel looked first from Doris to Jon then back to Doris, the confusion evident on his face.

"Having you two in the same room can't be good," he murmured under his breath, making Jon roll his eyes.

"The doctor thinks you can make a full recovery," Doris informed him. Daniel gave her a long look, his expression weary.

"Tell me, is this a weird joke or something?" asked Daniel loudly, trying to prop himself up on his elbows so he could sit up and move back on the bed.

"I told you to relax, Daniel. Trust me, this is as real as it gets," Jon said as he tried to help Daniel back into place on the hospital bed. Daniel weakly waved his arm at Jon while disconnecting the electrodes connected to his chest with the other. Doris attempted to hold his hand down, but he waved her off as well, a look of panic and annoyance spreading across his face.

"I don't need your help. I gotta get out of here," he said breathlessly as the beeping on one of the monitors began to increase in frequency.

"Daniel Pallson, you are not going anywhere. You need to rest. Now stop being a nuisance!" announced Doris sternly, reattaching one of the electrodes to his chest that he had just pulled off. Daniel paused in his tracks upon hearing Doris's words, but the next second he snapped.

"I need to go back to Boston. I have lots of work to do." The beeping now became almost continuous.

"When don't you ever have enough work?" Doris muttered bitterly.

At that moment, the nurse walked in and said in a raised voice, "Mr. Pallson, what do you think you are doing?" She hurried over to him, expertly reattaching monitors and electrodes while holding down both arms in a single vice grip. After they were all in place, she released his hands and took a step back.

"Seriously, Mr. Pallson, you have to rest. You're acting irresponsibly. You can't leave. Please understand," she told him firmly.

"You see, even the nurse agrees with us." Doris smirked, making Daniel more irritated. He didn't know how he felt about seeing her after all this time.

"Fine, but I want these people out of my room!" Daniel said, pointing to Jon and Doris. The nurse looked over at them and then back at Daniel, peering at him over her large spectacles.

"Oh, for heaven's sake, Daniel. You're acting like a child," Doris told him exasperatedly.

"Like I said, Nurse, I want them gone," he insisted, ignoring Doris's comment.

"Are you sure? These people have been at your side ever since you got out of surgery," she informed him, looking him in the eye as she did. She was an elderly, take-no-nonsense type of nurse, and Doris was grateful for her presence, as getting Daniel to listen to anyone could be a Herculean task.

"Are you telling me what to do?" he questioned, raising an eyebrow at her with a terse expression on his face. "I want to speak to the doctor. When will the doctor be here?"

"Momentarily. In the meanwhile, try not to disconnect any of these machines, or the nurses' station will think you have flat-lined, and I assure you there are plenty of patients who genuinely need our attention," the nurse responded before turning on her heel and leaving the room.

"I can't stay here. I need to get back to my office. I have work to do," Daniel announced after the nurse left, trying to lift himself up on his elbows once more.

"Stop this nonsense! You are in a hospital in Iceland. You have to rest," Doris said again.

"I want to see the doctor now!" Daniel shouted back. "Simon. Call Simon. Do you have his number?"

Just then, the doctor entered the room and smiled at Daniel. "What is this commotion all about? Mr. Pallson, I'm Doctor Einarsson, and I am happy to see you awake, and your signs are good, it would appear."

"Listen, Doc, I need to leave right away," Daniel told him, lying back down in frustration. He did not have the energy to keep himself propped up.

"Do you know why you are here?" Doctor Einarsson asked, flipping through the chart at the end of Daniel's hospital bed and reviewing his levels.

"They claim I had some sort of heart attack," Daniel replied, rolling his eyes and sighing deeply in frustration, the gravity of his condition being immaterial to him next to his work.

"And you were extremely lucky that you got to us this fast—."

Daniel held up his hand, silencing the doctor before saying dismissively, "Yeah, yeah, yeah. Call my private doctor. Doctor Walsh."

Doctor Einarsson looked at him in silence, giving him a long look, pausing for a few seconds before responding, "I have, and he agrees with me."

As Daniel comprehended the words the doctor told him, he settled back down in the hospital bed dejectedly, a look of resignation on his face. "Are you telling me I'm stuck in this hospital?"

"You have not been cleared, you need to rest, and you are not allowed to fly," Doctor Einarsson explained to him, placing his chart back and folding his hands in front of his chest.

"That's never gonna happen," scoffed Daniel.

"Mr. Pallson, the surgery saved your life. Do you realize how serious your condition was when you were brought in? Your arteries were blocked, and had you not been given medical attention at the right time we wouldn't even be having this conversation," the doctor said a little sternly, hoping the seriousness of his words would reach Daniel. He was used to workaholic patients like this who were usually entitled as well as incredibly rude.

"I don't care. Call Mr. Simon. He will square this out."

"The only person authorized to make such decisions is your wife, and she's right here," Doctor Einarsson said, gesturing to Doris, who was still standing by Daniel's side.

"She hasn't been with me for a few years. Just call my lawyer and get them out of here," Daniel told him, looking away. His words hurt Doris, even making Jon flinch. But Doris didn't react. She didn't want to show her emotions, not when Daniel was acting so ignorantly.

There was a knock at the door, and all four of them turned to see Simon and Phil enter the hospital room. Daniel sighed with relief and quipped, "Finally, a sight for sore eyes. Am I glad to see you two. You are the only ones I want here right now." He glared at Doris and Jon, who immediately gathered their belongings and left the hospital room, not wanting to do anything with company executives.

"Everything is going to be okay, Doris," said Jon as he exited the room. She was flushed in the face, walking briskly away from the room in anger. She stopped and turned to face Jon.

"He hasn't changed one bit. The intervening years have made him hard and bitter," she sighed.

"Yeah, well…" Jon shrugged, unable to excuse his brother's behavior.

"And then to see him. I just can't even stand the sight of that Greg Simon. The thought of him alone is enough to make me sick."

"Forget about him, and let Daniel be with them. Let's go to the farm and see Anna. It will make you feel better. She has been after me since last night to bring you home," Jon told her, putting his arm around her gently and steering her toward the exit.

CHAPTER 4
SUN SPOTS ON THE FARM

Pastor Jon drove through two enormous mountains with the glimmering ocean serving as their backdrop. The contrast was surreal, as the midday sun basked everything in an almost ethereal glow, reflecting off the water like encrusted jewels. Doris put her passenger-side window down and let the crisp, clean air blow through her hair. She inhaled deeply, taking it all in, enjoying her black local tea and remembering in her previous visits why it tasted so good then too.

She missed the rustic beauty of Iceland, especially the rural side, its wild beauty and endless space, a heavenly sight. The Icelandic countryside was made up of rivers, mountains, valleys, and waterfalls, but its volcanoes and glaciers, as well as hot springs, were what was so unique about it. Doris liked city life, but the natural and breathtaking beauty of this particular land, dotted with huge waterfalls, unbelievable beaches, and serene landscapes, invigorated her soul. She remembered when they were in

Connecticut and Thomas would ask about Iceland. Daniel would proudly tell him that wherever you went in Iceland, no matter the direction, you would always find something to be breathless about.

The contrast was surreal. From the blooming purple lupines so proud and tall, to the rough edges of the lava covered in thick soft green moss during the summer months with its black sand beaches that actually reminded her of the Big Island of Hawaii. She thought to herself how funny the irony of being in Iceland and thinking of a resemblance to Hawaii was.

They reached the farm not much later, and Jon parked his jeep outside the house but not in the garage. It was a sturdy yet beautifully built home made with wood and plenty of glass to let sunlight in. Its open floor plan was visible from the front, giving way to a comfortable yet modern interior littered with books, hand-woven tapestries, and comfortable armchairs, all centered around an indoor firepit.

Anna came to open the front door and waved excitedly as Doris got out of the jeep. Anna was tall with long ginger hair and a warm smile. Leading an active lifestyle with a healthy, farm-to-table diet slowed down her aging process tremendously, as she still managed to look half her actual age.

From the beginning, the two women had gotten along like a house on fire. Even when Jon and Daniel bickered, the two never let their respective spouses' differences affect their relationship.

"I am so glad you decided to come here!" squealed Anna, wrapping her arms around Doris and pulling her close.

"This is so much nicer than the city," Doris replied, hugging her back.

"I'm so glad to see you, Doris. I have missed you," Anna exclaimed.

"Likewise." Doris smiled.

"I am as hungry as a horse. What is there to eat?" Pastor Jon asked, giving Anna a peck on the cheek as he walked up to them.

"There are some ham and cheese sandwiches with whole grain mustard on the counter. Dinner will be a while, so please have a snack, or you are going to whine for the next four hours," laughed Anna while rolling her eyes.

"Which reminds me, it's almost time to feed the horses. Do you want to join me?" Anna asked Doris.

Doris had always loved horses and nodded her head enthusiastically.

"Why don't you girls go ahead? Doris, I will take your bags inside and grab a nibble in the meantime."

They both agreed and began the walk over to the stables. They crossed the meadow, and Doris took in the raw beauty of the ranch. When they reached, Doris spotted a stunning black stallion in his stall. She made her way to where he was and gently started stroking his long mane, talking to him slowly.

"This one is beautiful. What's his name?" Doris asked, not taking her eyes off the horse.

"He is called Blesi. One of our champions. Would you like to go out riding while you are here? Blesi loves a good romp," said Anna, seeing how naturally comfortable Dorris was around the horses.

"I would love that," she said, walking over to Anna and taking some bale to feed the horses with.

"How was it seeing Daniel after so long?" Anna asked.

"Awkward." Doris smiled ruefully.

"And what was his reaction?"

"Well, let's just say he couldn't wait to kick us out of the hospital room, and had he been up for it, he would have kicked us out himself," Doris told her.

"Sounds like Daniel," Anna chuckled, with Doris joining in after a beat.

* * *

Back at the hospital, Daniel looked over at the tray of food next to his bed in disgust. The broiled chicken and asparagus with bone broth were both tasteless and sad-looking. Even the pudding was runny and not at all appetizing.

Daniel inwardly cursed his condition for having to endure all this. He had already been here long enough to jeopardize his business, and staying here was no longer an option he could bear. He turned his attention back to the small TV in the corner, which had the Business Channel left on. Mr. Simon and Phil Wood walked into the room, the former carrying a big brown bag of takeout, which he handed over to Daniel, who practically snatched it from his grip.

"Why do all hospitals make bad food? It's like a universal conspiracy," Daniel quipped, gesturing toward the tray of uneaten food. He opened up the bag and inhaled deeply with a grin on his face. "Now that's what I'm talking about."

Daniel pulled out a double bacon cheeseburger so overloaded with grease that parts of the melty soft cheese fell back into the bag. He took a massive bite out of it and closed his eyes to chew. "Finally, some actual food instead of this space station stuff," he said when he swallowed.

"Is it okay to be eating that?" Mr. Simon commented, which Daniel completely ignored.

"Well, did you get those nincompoops to stop all the nonsense about me not leaving?" asked Daniel after finishing the massive burger in a few huge bites and discarding the wrapper in the bag.

"Yes, but it's gonna take a few days," Phil responded, wondering why Simon had agreed to bring the fatty burger for Daniel. They needed him as healthy as possible and as soon as possible at that. But deep down, he knew there was no denying Daniel Pallson something he wanted. And Simon was known not to back down from confrontation, except when it came to Daniel of course. It seemed he took it as his personal duty to agree to the man's every whim.

"A few days? Tell me an exact number," barked Daniel, not able to keep the annoyance out of his tone.

"A week," Phil replied.

"Are you kidding? That is unacceptable. Call the ambassador or the White House for that matter," Daniel replied, waving his arms around wildly as if it emphasized his urgency.

"That would not be a good idea, sir. You were not kidnapped, nor are you under any threat," Phil told him in a deadpan voice, his attitude implacable. "The doctor won't sign off on your discharge until you are ready to travel. No hospital would release a patient this fast. You know that."

"Damn insurance policies," Daniel grumbled under his breath while rolling his eyes. "There must be something that could be done. What about an air ambulance? I could travel in that and work from home?" he asked, sounding desperate.

"Air ambulances are not a solution. They don't have the range we need and are hardly bigger than the size of a small prop plane with medical equipment," Phil pointed out.

"Sir, I think it's best to work with the hospital. I know you hate hospitals, so I think we have reached a compromise, which we hope you accept. At least the hospital agrees with us, and you get your wish of working from home," Simon interjected, looking over hopefully at Daniel.

"I can't wait to hear this."

"It was actually your brother Jon who came up with this idea," Phil said as Daniel began laughing.

"Jon had an idea? I have got to hear this," he said, sitting up in the hospital bed.

"He offered for you to be at the family farm under Dr. Walsh's care while you recover," responded Simon.

Daniel stared at him, his mouth agape and shocked. For a while, there was silence, during which Simon and Phil both shifted uncomfortably in their spots.

"You call that an idea? You have got to be kidding," Daniel said finally, still unsure if his lawyer's words were an elaborate prank meant to give him another heart attack.

"Everyone has agreed to this, so it is up to you," Phil added.

"Yes, and you will be allowed some time for business calls and brief meetings with us. Trust us, sir, this is the best possible solution," Simon told him calmly, hoping to alleviate the negativity he had toward the idea, knowing that Daniel would never be able to conduct any business at the hospital.

"You're staying in Iceland too?" Daniel questioned without missing a beat. His voice was a little more accepting than it was before. Both men nodded affirmatively in response. "At the farm, huh?" They nodded again.

"Truth be told, I don't know which is worse, this hospital or having to be in the same place as my brother and the wife who deserted me," Daniel concluded, reflecting on what exactly that would mean for him to move in with his brother as opposed to being stuck at the hospital where he could not get anything done.

* * *

Jon sat in his rocking chair, thinking about the suggestion he had given to the hospital and Daniel's colleagues. He had asked Anna for permission, and she had agreed, which he was thankful for. Jon knew Daniel wouldn't easily agree to come to the farm, given how resentful he was. He was also worried about Doris and the way Daniel had reacted to her. It seemed his brother was still hurting and holding onto the past.

But perhaps this was a chance for all of them to rehash the past or even lay it to rest. Jon wanted his brother to see reason, and having him under his roof would not only make Daniel convalesce properly but might make him realize that commercializing natural resources was damaging to nature.

It wasn't going to be easy for any of them, yet Jon was ready to give it a try.

* * *

The next morning, Doris awoke to the sun trickling in through the bedroom curtain. She got out of bed, pulled the curtains back, and marveled at the view in front of her. Sheep were being herded into the far corner by an Alaskan Malamute, while the horses that had been bred to survive yet another season of the cold and dark now grazed happily in the lush, green expanse of the land now back to the land of the midnight sun. Doris slipped her robe on and went down to the kitchen. The smell of bacon and coffee wafted through the air, sparking her hunger.

"Good morning, Doris. Hope you slept well," Anna said as she saw her come down the steps. "Come down and pull up a seat. I am just finishing up making some pancakes."

"What a spread!" Doris exclaimed, looking at the platters of food laid out. There were scrambled eggs, a plate of crisp bacon, several varieties of bread arranged next to cheese, grapes, and a pot of honey. A basket on the side had fresh fruits that looked like they were just picked this morning. Anna was mixing together batter and a few drops of vanilla essence, which added to the symphony of smells that were coming from the breakfast table.

"Thank you. Everything you see here is from the farm. The eggs, milk, and honey are locally sourced. Even the butter is churned by hand," Anna responded, beaming.

"I really appreciate you guys doing this for me. It is so refreshing to be out here in the country. This farm holds a spot in my heart, one I forgot about until we drove up yesterday. It truly is magnificent here. And I have got to say, the food is pretty damn good too," Doris said in earnest to both of them, grinning at the variety in front of her.

"Why don't you both go outside and sit on the patio? Soak in some sunlight, Doris, and have your coffees outside," Anna suggested.

"Good idea, hon." Jon stood up and gave her a peck.

Sitting on the patio, Doris sighed blissfully, sipping her hot coffee.

"You okay with Daniel coming here?" Jon asked.

"It's your home, and I'm just a guest here," Doris shrugged.

"Still…"

"I want him to recover as quickly as possible. I still care, Jon, despite everything," she responded.

"Of course." He nodded.

"Did Phil say when Daniel would be arriving?" she asked, sitting down at the table and helping herself to some toast.

"No, probably later today."

Just then, two men got out of a cargo truck that had just parked outside and carried out a large hospital bed from the truck. There was medical equipment at the back of the truck, which they also began to slowly unload. A black SUV came up and parked behind it, followed by an ambulance.

"Or sooner," quipped Jon as he set his mug of coffee down and watched for his ailing brother to be wheeled into the home they once used to share so many years ago. Doris also stood up, a little anxious about the whole situation. Who would have thought they would all be back under the same roof under such circumstances?

Daniel looked around at the farm in front of him as he was wheeled out. The sun hit his eyes, and it took him a moment to adjust to the bright light surrounding him.

He looked at the sprawling ranch house with a sloping roof and raised patio. On his way, he had seen the farmland was well maintained, and it seemed Jon had added more acreage to it. He wasn't sure how, but he had heard that the farm was profiting.

Now, being here, a place where he had such beautiful memories, made him emotional. He didn't want to feel this way, but a part of him was happy to see that Jon hadn't made major architectural changes to the main homestead.

"Wow, I can't believe I used to mow this whole farm every weekend. It would take all of Saturday and part of

Sunday," he told the paramedic, who was helping him into the wheelchair in front of the house.

"Damn, that's a lot of lawn to mow," the paramedic replied in amazement.

"It sure is. My father paid me three kronos each time I cut it," Daniel smiled, fondly recalling the hours he spent under the sun in his youth.

"Only three kronos? That can't be right."

"That seemed like a pretty good deal for me back then," Daniel chuckled. "Back then, pretty much everything seemed like a good deal, I suppose," he mused.

As the paramedic wheeled Daniel toward the patio, his smile fell, and his body tensed up, seeing Doris looking at him and Jon making his way toward him. Daniel squared his shoulders and readied himself for what he was sure was going to be quite a reckoning in the coming days.

CHAPTER 5
NEW FACES, OLD PLACES

Standing on the patio, Doris saw Daniel's expressions hardening as Jon greeted the paramedic and slightly nodded to Daniel, who didn't bother acknowledging his brother. She decided to join Jon, and together they greeted Doctor Walsh as Simon and Phil emerged out of the black SUV. In the center was Daniel, assisted by a paramedic and a nurse from the hospital.

"This is a beautiful place you have here," said Dr. Walsh, admiring the woodwork of the house before looking over the lush green expanse surrounding them.

"Thanks, it's been in the family since they built it in the 1940s," Jon told him, after which there was an awkward silence coupled with an almost palpable tension between Daniel and his brother. He would not even look up and acknowledge either Jon or Doris, making everyone involved rather uncomfortable as a result. After a while, Dr. Walsh cleared his throat and broke the silence by asking if all the medical equipment needed for Daniel's stay had arrived.

"Yes, everything has been set up," Jon replied. There was still no reaction from Daniel, who kept looking ahead, blatantly ignoring it each time Doris glanced in his direction, expecting him to say something.

"Which part of the house have you had it all set up in?" questioned the doctor. Jon looked in Daniel's direction and answered, "Actually, I thought your old bedroom would be best."

"My old bedroom? You have got to be kidding me," gasped Daniel at Jon's statement, immediately bolting upright in his stretcher.

"It is on the first floor and is the easiest access in the whole house." Jon shrugged. The doctor nodded in agreement.

"Good choice, can we take a look?" asked Dr. Walsh.

Jon led the way into the house, followed by Dr. Walsh and the rest of the party. Daniel shot a look at Simon and Phil that clearly was pleading with them to get him out of there. The two men shrugged and looked away, not pleased with the situation either.

The paramedic pushed Daniel into his old room, where another nurse was setting up the rest of the medical equipment. The room had been sterilized beforehand. Daniel looked at the IV stand, monitor, and other paraphernalia before taking in the rest of the room. He glanced around the space he had not seen for over two decades. It had been remodeled somewhat but still looked enough the same to elicit a strong wave of nostalgia within Daniel. The bookshelves and the chest drawers that he had grown up with were exactly how he remembered them. The walls seemed to have been repainted in the recent past, yet the wall hangings and framed pictures were the same. A bittersweet smile played on his lips as his eyes passed over the loose floorboard where he used to hide any mischievous or private items from others. He shook his head and quickly came back to protesting against his stay at the farm.

"This is insane. I can't stay here," he grumbled.

Doris replied firmly, "You will be fine here." "Unbelievable. The same bookcase and drawers," he said under his breath, which Doris ignored.

Doctor Walsh entered the room and went over the equipment setup. "This is just the right place for you to recover. The fresh air and serene landscape will be quite invigorating for you. Much better than the hospital, I believe."

"I'll survive. What other choice do I have?" Daniel grimaced.

Daniel continued looking around at the four walls he had spent so much time in, unable to block out the flood of memories that were coming back to him each time his eyes settled on something familiar from the past. The paramedic and nurse lifted him from his stretcher and moved him to the hospital bed that had been brought in. After he was settled in the bed, they wheeled the stretcher out back to the ambulance to make more room before attaching Daniel to the various heart monitors and drips he needed to be on.

Daniel closed his eyes wearily, feeling the exhaustion of the move combined with annoyance at the presence of so many people. He wanted to be left alone, especially by Jon and Doris, so he kept his eyes closed. Jon and Doris took that as their cue to leave and walked out of his room, followed by Dr. Walsh, leaving the nurse to continue her work.

After a few moments, Daniel opened his eyes. "Are they gone?" he asked in a low whisper.

"Yes," the nurse replied.

Daniel sighed and looked up, staring at the ceiling. He was frightened. For the first time in a long time, ever since the power and money had trickled into his life, he was afraid, a large reason for that being his lack of control over the situation. His decisions and choices were not his own, and instead he had to rely on other people, which was something he had cut out of his life many years ago. The helplessness was almost more than he could bear, and he quickly blinked back tears while tilting his head toward the window, hoping the green land outside would be enough to calm him down, enough to stop the flow of tears and allow him to regain his composure.

He couldn't break down now, not when he needed his wits about him. While he was physically in a weakened state, he couldn't also let himself become emotionally vulnerable. But seeing his brother and estranged wife and living with them at such close quarters truly baffled him.

* * *

Doris, Simon, Phil, and Jon were sitting around the kitchen table as Anna poured out coffee into each of their mugs, leaving the milk and sugar in the middle of the table to add to according to their preferences.

"Would you like anything for breakfast?" Anna asked the men.

"No, thank you. I ate on the plane," Doctor Walsh told her.

"We're good, thanks," said Phil.

Anna nodded and sat back on the table next to Jon. Simon was watching the news on his phone, leaning his face on one hand while propping the phone up with the other.

"We have breaking news regarding Daniel 'Big Deal' Pallson, who was hospitalized in critical condition in Iceland four days ago. Let's go to Susan Hernandez, who is still there. Susan?"

Susan stood in front of the hospital where Daniel was admitted before being moved to the farm.

"It's been reported that Mr. Pallson left the Central Reykjavik Hospital this morning in an ambulance. According to eyewitnesses, Mr. Pallson looked frail. Following the cardiovascular event he endured, his shares in his company have been hit hard with volatility as speculation grows regarding his successor or even takeover. And it is not helping that there have been no comments from the company." Susan held onto her earpiece, holding her hand up before continuing, "And this just in, the exchange has suspended trading for the company."

"Oh, you have got to be freakin' kidding me," Simon said, slamming his hand on the kitchen top, startling both Jon and Doris.

"This is not good people… Not good at all!" Phil cursed.

"People, please keep this from Mr. Pallson, at least until I can do more tests," Doctor Walsh implored while Simon got up, pacing up and down, trying to make a call.

"What does this mean?" asked Doris, looking from Phil to Doctor Walsh.

"It means," said Phil, shaking his head, "that if Daniel does not get better, we are in huge trouble."

At that moment, Simon came and sat back down, but as soon as he did, his phone began ringing. He quickly picked up the call.

"Ted, I just saw it. Yes, I know, but still…" he said and paused, listening intently to the reply from the other end. "Let me ask the doctor." Simon turned toward Doctor Walsh and looked him in the eye, "We need Daniel to make a statement. It can be done on the phone if that helps."

"I strongly advise against it. He needs total rest," Dr. Walsh replied.

"So is the stock volatility that could have a huge negative impact on many people all over the world," Simon argued, still holding his hand over the receiver of the phone.

"We can see in the morning. Maybe, just maybe, he can do a quick interview session from his room," sighed Dr. Walsh as Simon shrugged in agreement.

"Works for us," Simon answered, going back to his phone call. "Ted, if the doctor approves, tell them they can have an exclusive with Susan. Just two minutes convincing her he is fine and expected to go back to the office soon."

"Do I have any say in this?" asked Doris crossly, knowing that news like this could potentially be life-threatening to Daniel in the state he was in.

"He has to make a statement. You saw the news," Phil told her in a calm, cool voice, completely unaffected by how upset she was by the situation.

"Is it ever enough with you people?" she snapped back at him hotly before gathering her shawl and marching back upstairs to the room she was staying in.

Once in her room, Doris closed the door shut a little loudly. She was furious with Greg Simon. The man was still as insufferable as ever and seemed to lack even an ounce of humanity. He was the leading accomplice to Daniel's never-ending and long-time obsession with business dealings to set aside any personal side of life's problematic emotions. The more she thought about the past events, the more exasperated she felt.

* * *

Daniel woke up startled. He'd barely had a few minutes of rest when he heard a loud bang and then raised voices. He slowly pushed himself up, trying to listen to what was going on, but all he could hear were muffled sounds.

Daniel's throat felt parched, and staying in the room was making him claustrophobic. He gingerly tried to get up, failing in the first few attempts, but with willpower he was finally able to get out of bed.

"Can't you guys, or any other shareholder, make the statement instead of Daniel? Is it imperative that he do it? You all saw how weak he is," Jon argued.

"He's the face of the company, so only his word will work," Phil said emphatically.

"His medical treatments supersede any other decision, including the stock market. Understood?" Dr. Walsh interjected and told Phil, raising his voice slightly.

"What is going on in New York?" Daniel said from behind them, and they all spun around to see him enter the kitchen in his wheelchair, the IV drip stand rolling along. His face looked haggard, and the perspiration on his forehead showed how much effort it must have taken him to get out of bed and make it out of the room.

Simon also came back into the kitchen, looked up from his phone, and was taken aback to see Daniel sitting in there in a chair.

"Sir, you are up?" Simon asked him, still surprised by his sudden appearance.

"I couldn't sleep," he told them, waving his hand as if to dismiss the question.

"With all due respect, you need to stay in bed!" the doctor told him, moving over to wheel him back to his room. Daniel shot him a look that made him stop where he was.

"I said, what is going on in New York?"

Everyone looked at each other nervously, wondering how to break the news to him and contemplating whether they should.

CHAPTER 6
THE INTERVIEW

The next day, Jon was sitting at his desk, logging some records for the farm's output and water usage. He kept a meticulous journal of all the numbers and management needed to go into maintaining the farm. Upon his son Magnus's insistence, Jon had switched to keeping track of the data on his computer instead of a handwritten, worn-out journal from which he was uploading previous records.

"I don't know why you have to upload the new data. Why can't you just move forward with the new numbers?" his wife asked as she folded laundry on the bed and put it away in the large walk-in closet attached to the room. There were vases of freshly cut flowers scattered all throughout the room and closet, encasing the sunlit area in a floral cloud of scent. Anyone who came to visit commented on how it looked like something out of a catalog because of the ceiling-to-floor glass windows that looked over the entirety of the farm. A cozy yet chic interior was designed by Anna, who had successfully married style with comfort with its off-white and cool-beige tones.

"Because then I won't be able to compare the changes," explained Jon, peering over his spectacles at the screen. At that moment, a ten-year-old boy burst into their bedroom and nuzzled his way into Jon's lap.

"Dagur! I thought you guys were not coming until this weekend?" Jon said, laughing as he turned the computer off with his free hand and tickled the child with the other.

Anna spun around and opened her arms wide as Dagur came running into them, almost knocking her over with a tight bear hug.

"Happy birthday, Grandma!" he said, kissing her delicately on the cheek as Magnus, his father, walked into the room.

"Surprise! Happy birthday, Mom!" Magnus said to Anna with a huge grin plastered to his face, reaching over and giving her a hug. "I got you some flowers, but I think you may have enough," he chuckled, handing her a bouquet of the native summer dainty holtasoley flowers as he noted the dozens of flowers already sprinkled among the vases in the house.

"You know how your father gets on birthdays." Anna smiled. "You came early for my birthday! What a treat! I thought you guys were due on Friday! Will you be staying?" she asked, looking up at Magnus.

"Sorry, Ma, I promised Erla I would be back by tonight," replied Magnus.

"I will be staying," interjected Dagur with a giggle, hiding behind the hem of his grandmother's skirt.

"Of course you will be," Anna said, pulling the cloth away as he laughed.

"I can't wait to go fishing with Grandpa," Dagur told her before running to Jon to confirm that they would, in fact, go fishing as soon as possible.

"So, heard you have a full house?" Magnus asked, raising an eyebrow slightly and looking at his father.

"Yup, your Uncle Daniel is staying with us," Jon answered, taking his spectacles off and placing them back in their case near the computer.

"Dad, how on earth did this happen? And do you really think it's a good idea?" Magnus questioned, turning to face his father and looking him in the eye, dumbfounded.

"It is the best solution for everyone after the heart attack."

"Call it what you like," Magnus commented before Anna quickly changed the subject, sensing the tension in the room.

"Aunt Doris will be so glad to see you both," she told Magnus and Dagur.

"Where is she? I haven't seen her in ages," Magnus asked, still processing the fact that his uncle, who he had last seen fifteen years ago, was in the room downstairs. When he had heard his uncle was in Iceland starting a commercial venture, he knew old resentments would surface. But he never envisaged him having a heart attack and coming to the family home for rest. The whole idea had seemed preposterous.

"Come here, Dagur. Let's go see Aunt Doris," Jon said, getting up from his chair and taking Dagur by the hand.

"You coming?" he paused to ask his son, who was still frowning. Magnus nodded. Jon and Dagur walked down the stairs as Anna and Magnus trailed behind them.

Doris was in the kitchen when they went down, making herself some coffee and smearing a bagel with some cream cheese.

"Hello, Aunt Doris," Magnus greeted her.

"My goodness, is that you, Magnus? How long has it been?" asked Doris when she saw them. He walked over and gave her a hug.

"A long time, Aunt Doris. Good to see you," he replied as he pulled away.

"And who are you, young man?" she asked, bending down so she was at face level with Dagur.

"My name is Dagur," he replied seriously, holding his hand out for her to shake. She took his hand in hers and could not help but smile. Doris bent down and looked right into Dagur's eyes.

"He looks like your spitting image, Magnus, though he has his mother's eyes," Doris commented as she pinched Dagur on the cheek as he blushed.

"And also his mother's sense of adventure." Magnus smirked, ruffling his son's hair. "That coffee smells great." Dagur quickly began to get fidgety. "And I want a snack!"

They all sat down to catch up. Anna took out some bread, cheese, and mayonnaise, buttering the outside of the slices before adding the mayo and cheese, grilling them on a flat top before cutting them in half.

"That smells so yummy, Grandma. Can I have the first one?" Dagur asked, standing close to where she was and looking into the pan.

"Of course, you can. But first, the secret ingredient!" Anna told him, pulling the bread pieces apart and sticking sliced pickles between the tunnels of gooey cheese.

"Why didn't you add the pickles before grilling them?" Dagur asked, swallowing a massive bite while it was still steaming slightly.

"Chew your food," Magnus scolded, eagerly taking the next plate from his mother's hands.

"Because this is the only way they will stay crunchy! Now go on and give everyone a sandwich if you are done with yours," Anna said as Dagur began passing them around. Doris had already poured out mugs of coffee for the adults, while Anna found a big bag of chips to pass around along with the grilled cheese sandwiches.

"Can I go see Daddy's uncle now? I wanna see if he looks like Grandpa," Dagur asked.

"Not now, Dagur. He is resting. Maybe later I'll take you to meet him," Jon placated him.

"Quite some family reunion, huh… Who would have thought?" Magnus commented, surveying the scene.

"Yes! It's been an interesting development," said Doris wryly, rolling her eyes as they heard raised voices coming from Daniel's room.

"I just hope you all realize what you've taken on." Magnus looked at his father, who gave him a silencing look. Even at this age, when Magnus was also a father, Pastor Jon had the ability to intimidate his son.

* * *

Meanwhile, in Daniel's room, there was a fair bit of commotion. Mr. Simon paced up and down the room nervously as Phil Wood sat in the chair opposite Daniel's bed, looking at his phone.

"Be brief, no reason to offer any extra explanation. All we have to do is convince them you are okay and working hard," Mr. Simon told him as Daniel shot him an annoyed look.

"I know how to handle the press," sighed Daniel before beginning to cough.

"Normally, yes, I would say you do," commented Phil.

"I am fine, really," Daniel quickly replied as soon as he caught his breath.

"They promised to stay on script, only focusing on your ability to go back to work," Mr. Simon reassured him, stopping his pacing and looking at Daniel.

"Do you really expect them to keep their promises?" Daniel asked incredulously, which made Mr. Simon start pacing nervously once again.

"I know it's the press, but I think we can trust Susan," he replied softly.

"Have I taught you nothing? The press can never be trusted. They always have a hidden agenda, so I really doubt that they can be trusted, but we'll see," Daniel said.

"Dr. Walsh was very explicit that it should be a short, quick interview," Phil reminded them.

Daniel sat up in a chair in the bedroom and said, "I am doing this interview even if it kills me."

* * *

At the studio, Susan Hernandez sat in the anchor chair. Her powder-blue blazer, perfectly blow-dried hair, and carefully applied makeup gave her an air of boss-lady persona. This particular news story was making waves, and she had caught public attention, so milking this opportunity was a must for her. Behind her chair, in the background, was the logo of Daniel Pallson's company. Graphics showed that the stock price had dropped considerably since Daniel had fallen ill.

"Good morning, everyone. We will start the newscast today with a phone interview with Mr. Daniel Pallson, who recently had a double bypass and was hospitalized in his native Iceland." The screen split to reveal Daniel, who was

Zooming from his family farm where he grew up. "Hello, Mr. Pallson, Susan Hernandez from ENBC."

"Hello, Susan, and thank you for having me," Daniel said in a clear voice, smiling slightly in a charming, almost beguiling way despite his condition.

"Thank you for coming today. The first question is obvious. How are you, sir?" she asked, her eyes scanning to see any cracks in his façade.

"I'm doing well. At least that's what my doctor tells me."

"So the rumors are not true?" Susan pushed on, noticing the oxygen cylinder that was barely visible behind Daniel's bed on the camera.

"I think my demise has been strongly exaggerated," Daniel chuckled as Susan smiled in response. "I want to use the opportunity to thank the medical team in Iceland. They did a great job."

"Which leads me to my next question. With you being still in Iceland and not in your office, should shareholders be concerned?" Susan interrogated, the smile quickly fading from her face.

"Of course not. And frankly I cannot remember the last time I took a few days off. Staying in Iceland will only rejuvenate me," Daniel told her in a calm, collected tone.

"According to the news, you are stirring things up a bit in Iceland," Susan stated, clearly trying to egg Daniel on in one way or another.

"I don't think I ever developed something that didn't stir things up, but in the end it usually works out," he replied.

"Aren't you restricting public access to your river?" Susan continued as chaos erupted behind the camera back in Daniel's room.

Mr. Simon was on the phone trying to maintain composure while hissing down the phone line, "I knew they would do that. Tell them I will disconnect the phone if they keep this up. Tell 'em now!"

Daniel was not happy with the question and all the assumptions connected to it but kept his composure nicely. Phil was juggling between two phones while Dr. Walsh glared at everyone in the room.

"First of all, there are plenty of rivers in Iceland. And if one wants to fish in our river, he or she is always welcome," Daniel responded, his voice still incredibly calm, almost commanding. On the screen, the viewers could see Susan holding her earpiece as she was being fed live information.

"It's well known, Mr. Pallson, that you hardly do interviews. Our source from the hospital tells us you are still in serious condition and are not allowed to travel. How do you respond to that?"

"With what's going on in the world, do people really care about an old guy like me? Really?" Daniel retorted, not missing a beat, the charming smile still on his lips.

"With all due respect, sir, you can move the world financial markets. You did not answer my question."

"I believe I answered that question earlier—" Daniel began before Susan cut him off and interrupted him with another question.

"So, is our source wrong?"

"Rumors are what they are, rumors. Have a good day, Ms. Hernandez. I need to attend another meeting," Daniel replied a little more curtly than he had before. He hung up the call and looked in the direction of Phil and Mr. Simon.

"I told you these people had a hidden agenda. And how the hell did they know so much about my condition?" he asked angrily.

"I will handle this," replied Phil, dialing a number on his phone and leaving the room, followed closely by Mr. Simon, whose phone began ringing. They passed Pastor Jon, who was just entering Daniel's bedroom. Daniel looked at him and groaned. His estranged brother, whose place he was trapped in, was the last person he wanted to see right then. "I am in the middle of something, Jon."

"Don't worry, I am not staying long," Jon chided as Dr. Walsh also left the room, leaving the two brothers alone. The tension between them was almost palpable as Jon moved awkwardly toward Daniel's chair.

"Since you were in and out so quickly for Mom's funeral, I didn't get a chance to give you these things Mom wanted you to have." Jon handed Daniel a box, and he sat up and gasped as he took out an aged picture of John Wayne.

"Oh my goodness! My John Wayne picture. I had it on my wall since I was about ten," exclaimed Daniel.

"Used to go to the cinema every chance we got," commented Jon, thinking back fondly. Daniel then pulled out another picture, one from the fifties, around the time when their parents first met.

"Wow. Is that from the US base?" asked Daniel.

"Yes, she was wearing her American Navy nurse uniform, and Dad's in his civil mechanic's garb."

"I remember that truck. Seems like another lifetime," sighed Daniel, going through the other memorabilia in the box. There was a long silence, after which Jon finally said, "Why did you stop coming?"

Daniel looked at him and shook his head. He put the pictures back in the box and placed it on the side. "You know why."

"No, not really. I know we had our differences, but still… I can't pinpoint the place where it all started going downhill," Jon replied.

"Come on, Jon, not now, okay? I'm too tired to have this conversation," Daniel told him warily.

Jon said nothing as he turned and left the room, passing Dr. Walsh as he reentered to check on Daniel's vitals.

CHAPTER 7
COMING BACK HOME

THE SERENE LANDSCAPE of sloping green hills and dull-blue sky with shades of dusk reflected on the calm surface of Lake Þingvallavatn. Pastor Jon had taken Dagur out for fishing as promised, and now they were at one of the most famous lakes for fishing in Iceland. Lake Þingvallavatn was close to the capital city, Reykjavik, and just a few miles away from the farm too. The beautiful and enriching surroundings made fishing a surreal experience there. Jon had been wanting to bring Dagur there for a long time, knowing well that his grandson would love it.

Pastor Jon liked the lake. Despite it being a popular spot, it was still secluded enough for him to enjoy the landscape. He remembered how much they all loved coming here for family picnics, although Salmon Valley was their ultimate spot. Thinking about it made him flinch, as it gutted him to think how that beautiful piece of land would soon be commercialized.

"I thought you were going to take me to Lake Myvatn for fly-fishing," Dagur spoke, breaking into Jon's thoughts.

"I told you we're having a barbecue in the evening with the fresh salmon and trout we catch. I'll take you to Lake Myvatn soon too, I promise," Jon told him. Then, as an afterthought, he continued, "Do you know it's a popular geothermal area with freshwater systems?"

"Yeah, Mom told me it's a really cool place," Dagur said enthusiastically.

Seeing his grandson so excited pleased Jon, and he was glad to be out of the farm for a while. The vibe around the house was tense. Everyone was walking on eggshells. And after his terse exchange with Daniel, Jon really needed a break. Going fishing with his grandson was just the escape he needed.

"Look, Grandpa, we've caught something," Dagur jumped excitedly and pointed at the fishing line. Jon immediately reeled the fishing line in and, with immense force, was able to lift the fishing line.

"Oh my God, it's so big…" Dagur exclaimed, looking at a three-feet-long salmon. Even Jon was impressed, for one rarely ever caught such a big salmon. The usuals were approximately twenty inches or so.

"Seems like we're going to have quite a feast tonight," Jon winked at Dagur.

Later, they placed their catch of the day in the cooler they brought and packed up their fishing gear. Traipsing through beautiful fields, the duo seemed happy. The evening twilight threw a beautiful golden light on the green foliage around them, the sky turning a darker shade of pink and purple.

"Hey, son, aren't you gonna ask me your usual question?" Jon asked.

"What's that?"

"What's that? You know, what's for dinner?" Jon chuckled.

"Oh, yes! Hey, Grandpa, what's for dinner?" Dagur asked.

"I thought you'd never ask. It's salmon. The best salmon in the world," Jon told him.

They both laughed as they continued down the road.

* * *

"Hey, do you want any help making the salad?" Anna asked Doris, who was busy chopping the lettuce for the Caesar salad she was making.

"For the last time, Anna, I don't need help. It's just a salad. You've been doing so much for us, even making apple pie for dinner. The least I can do is make the salad and set the table. Here, why don't you just sit down and have some white wine? It's good to relax sometimes," Doris teased.

"I know. That's what Jon keeps telling me. But in all honesty, I can't keep still," Anna told her as she sat down.

Doris quickly made the dressing for the salad, added the fresh lettuce, and tossed it, whereas Anna finished her wine glass. Afterward, they both set the table for dinner.

"Why don't you finish up setting up the rest while I go check on the boys?" Anna told Doris and went to check up on the men who were on barbecue duty.

"I still can't believe you caught such a nice salmon," Magnus admired the fish while filleting it.

"Dagur caught it, not me," Jon told him.

"Yeah, Dad, that's right," Dagur chirped.

"How's the dinner coming along?" Anna asked as Jon flipped the grill.

"Just about done. Why don't you call our guests for dinner?" Jon suggested.

* * *

Daniel was not at the barbecue. Instead, he opted to sit on the outside patio of his room, sipping on a cup of tea and reading a financial newspaper. He had seen Jon and Dagur come in with their catch, and a wistful expression had fallen on his face. Seeing Jon happy with his family made Daniel's heart ache, a bitterness coiling inside. Sometimes, despite having every luxury at his disposal, he thought of the gone days and his only son, now dead.

He had heard about the barbecue but decided to eat in his room instead. He had no interest in playing house with the family. Besides, the interview had completely exhausted him, and he had no energy left to socialize any further.

The nurse had come in earlier to check up on him and, afterward, helped him come sit outside and take in the scenic beauty of the farm.

Just as he was turning the page, he heard footsteps and looked up to see a woman walking by. She was dressed smartly in a black turtleneck, black pants, and tan overcoat. Her bob-cut hairstyle suited her sharp features. Daniel didn't recognize her and tried recalling if he had ever seen her before, but it didn't seem likely. Perhaps she was a friend of Jon and Anna's.

"Hello." Sensing his gaze, she waved and greeted him in a friendly voice.

"Excuse me, do I know you?" Daniel asked, perplexed.

"We haven't been properly introduced, but I think you do know of me," Adams spoke, her intelligent eyes shining brightly.

Daniel looked at her closely, although he was still confused.

"I am Dr. Adams, a friend of Doris's," she finally introduced herself.

Hearing her name, Daniel's expression changed. His mouth turned into a thin line, a frown wrinkling his forehead.

"Oh, of course. I know of you. The infamous Dr. Adams. Doris's guru," Daniel said condescendingly.

"Good God! Spiritual advisor. Counselor, reverend, friend, but not guru, please. It sounds too off." Dr. Adams showed her displeasure.

Daniel rolled his eyes, bemused at the woman's flippant answer. All of a sudden, he turned hostile.

"What are you doing here?" he asked angrily.

"Mr. Pallson, Doris asked me to come visit here for a few days," she replied, deciding to ignore his rudeness. She gave him a break, figuring very well that he was bedridden and recuperating from such a big scare.

"Why? Did she have a heart attack too?"

"No, but she wanted me here for support, I suppose." Dr. Adams shrugged.

"Oh, yes, you and your support. Look what good it did to us," he said bitterly.

"Can we at least try to be civil to one another then?" she requested.

"How can I be civil to the one person I remember after our son died who misguided my wife to the extent that it created a wedge between us? Somehow, you convinced Doris that, oh, it was meant to be and to carry on as usual," Daniel sneered.

"Mr. Pallson, how dare you describe our difficult years of work with such a greedy simplification? I can see you're still embittered, and there's no reasoning with you.

I must be on my way," Dr. Adams spoke resignedly. She could tolerate his rudeness, but this person was downright insulting her belief system.

"It was a pleasure finally meeting you after all these years," he spoke sarcastically.

"The pleasure was all mine," she emphasized then stalked past him, whereas Daniel continued to sit on the patio, his mood sour after meeting with Dr. Adams. He blamed the woman for brainwashing Doris and making her seek spirituality instead of seeking comfort with her own husband during the turbulent times that came in their marriage, eventually separating the two.

* * *

It was sundown, and Jon had switched on the garden lights as well as the overhead lights once the barbecue was out in the garden, and they had set the table there since the weather was lovely.

There was smoked salmon, grilled trout, fresh oysters, Caesar salad, mashed potatoes, and gravy, as well as fried fish on the menu, and later, a Icelandic dessert delicacy of a layer cake with plums and cream to be served with homemade vanilla ice cream, one of Anna's specialties.

Once Reverend Adams had joined everyone, Doris had made the introductions, and now Dr. Adams was immersed in a conversation with Magnus. Everyone seemed to be in good spirits, and after the wine had been poured into each glass, Jon stood up and cleared his throat.

"I would like to welcome everyone here tonight and wish that your stay here is comfortable and to your liking, considering the circumstances," he said, raising the glass.

"And before we start on supper, let's just pray together for Mr. Pallson's health as well as for prosperity for all of us and thank our Lord for this beautiful night," Dr. Adams suggested.

"I love it. Midnight sun, Icelandic cookout. Something this New York City slicker never thought he would experience. It's so gorgeous out here. Amazing," Mr. Simon said.

"Yes, this is where Anna and I like to bring our guests. Where is Phil?" Jon asked.

"He had to go back to the East Coast at his earliest. Something came up. I forgot to tell you he looked for you before he left," Mr. Simon explained.

"That's too bad," Anna said.

"I do know one thing though. He and I agreed that Daniel coming here was the right thing to do. This really would help him recover faster," Mr. Simon said.

"Speaking of him, have you delivered Daniel and the nurse's dinners to the house?" Jon asked Anna.

"Yes, I took the tray in. He was having broth and grilled salmon along with the salad. I'll take in the pie later," replied Anna before saying, "Would anyone like some more wine?"

"On a beautiful day like this, why not?" Dr. Adams smiled and raised her glass.

"This fish is delicious, nicely done, Dad," Magnus praised his father.

"Oh, yes. It's so fresh, much tastier than what you get in some of the fanciest places in the States," Mr. Simon also joined in the praise.

Just then, the pastor's phone rang, and he answered.

"Hello." He listened to the person on the line. "Oh yes, he is still here." Pastor Jon listened some more.

"Now, like in half an hour? Okay, I'll tell him. He'll be over there right after he finishes his dinner. Okay? Thanks," he finished the call and hung up, looking right at Magnus.

"That was the nurse. Daniel says he would be happy to see you," he told Magnus, who looked a little dazed upon hearing this.

CHAPTER 8
PICTURE OF THE PAST

Magnus finished what was remaining on the plate and picked it up to put it into the sink. His stomach groaned slightly, as he had eaten more than he normally would, but the fish was so incredibly fresh and well-cooked that he could not stop the fork from lifting bites to his mouth. It was only when the top button of his jeans pressed into him that he realized it was time to stop. For some reason, he felt anxious to see his Uncle Daniel, who he had not seen or interacted with in any way since his cousin Thomas's funeral nearly twenty years ago. After dinner, he had walked to Daniel's room on the first floor and now stood before the closed door, fidgeting and mustering up the courage.

He finally knocked on Daniel's bedroom door before hearing the response, "Come in."

Daniel was sitting propped up on his bed, holding what looked like a thick docket of a business report. He closed it and put it down next to him when Magnus walked in.

"Magnus, look at you. A grown young man," Daniel beamed as Magnus walked up to him and held his hand out for Daniel to shake. Despite having just survived a nearly fatal heart attack, Magnus noted that he had a firm, confident handshake that had been rehearsed over and over. Magnus sat down on the chair next to Daniel's bed and looked over at him. It hit him just how much his uncle had aged over the last two decades.

"I don't particularly think thirty-eight years is still young," chuckled Magnus. His uncle was always fond of him until they stopped talking, and he remembered what a flair Daniel had for being incredibly charismatic.

"When someone as old as me tells you that you are young, you better believe it, kid," Daniel said before beginning to cough. Magnus instantly stood up, got a glass of water from the bedside, and handed it to Daniel, who gulped it down appreciatively.

A few minutes later, he caught his breath and continued with what he was saying. "I hear you went into law. That is a fine and respectable profession. What kind of law did you pursue?"

"Mostly commercial real estate law. My office and home are in London, so I am based out of there. We come as much as we can so that Dagur can see his grandparents frequently. He really loves it out here. London can get a bit stuffy when you have this to compare it to," Magnus said, gesturing to the marvelous view that was visible through Daniel's window, which had the curtains drawn back, allowing the Icelandic sun to stream in and illuminate the space through the lush green land that seemed to be teeming with life.

"It is quite a view," agreed Daniel solemnly. "So London, huh? It's one of my favorite cities in the whole world." There were a few moments of silence during which Daniel noticed Magnus staring at the ring on his hand.

"Wow, you still wear that ring. The American football championship ring. I remember that from when I was a kid. I thought it was the coolest thing I ever saw," mused Magnus, remembering how it was just as shiny all those years ago.

"Yeah, for my Ohio State championship team," Daniel said fondly, admiring it in the light.

"Oh, of course," Magnus exclaimed, smacking his palm on his forehead. "I remember how good you were. All-American kicker, if I am not mistaken?"

"You remember that?" Daniel asked with disbelief as he sat up a little straighter so he could see Magnus better.

"Dad would tell me all the time. He was very proud of that. Actually, he would tell everybody about it," Magnus added.

"Oh, wow. He told you all that?" Daniel asked, still registering what Magnus had said.

"And how you passed up kicking in the pros to start your business in America, which you couldn't wait to do."

"That is right. He told you that too?" Daniel asked. It just dawned on him how much his brother spoke about him.

"And anybody who would listen," smiled Magnus.

Again, a certain silence filled the air as Magnus noticed that Daniel was a little choked up by this revelation. Daniel reached over and picked up an old photograph off his side table that was piled with the things his mother had left him. Magnus was amazed by what he saw.

"Do you know who that is?" asked Daniel as Magnus stared at the picture with a soft smile on his face.

"Isn't that me and Thomas?"

"It sure is. You were about fourteen, I guess. Look at you two looking so damn happy. Were you boys as happy as you looked?" There was a tone of melancholy and sadness in Daniel's voice as he asked that, and he felt heavy with emotion. These were feelings he tried keeping closed in a box for as long as possible, hoping they would not reach his conscious mind during his day-to-day life, but sitting there in a hospital bed, looking at his brother's son, and remembering his own was a lot for Daniel to handle.

"We sure were. I can remember that time from this picture. I even remember the goofy hat he was wearing. Thomas and I always had fun when we were able to see each other. Especially when we went fishing," he told Daniel gently, sifting through his own nostalgia as he did.

"You know, it's interesting. Just looking at you now, I forgot how much of a Pallson I remember you looking like as a kid."

"I remember people telling Thomas how much he looked like you," responded Magnus, realizing that his uncle was tearing up slightly as there was a crack in his voice when he spoke.

"That is right. You remember that? Just think what he would look like if he was alive today and be a fine young man like you."

Magnus shifted uncomfortably in his seat, not knowing how to answer. He looked outside Daniel's window and stayed silent for a minute. "I bet he would still look like you."

"I bet he would too," said Daniel, picking up the picture again and handing it to Magnus. "I want you to have this, Magnus. And when you look at it, which I hope is a lot, will you do one thing for me? Remember how happy you and Thomas were back then. You two were happy then, right?"

"Yes, I know we definitely were both happy then."

Daniel sat back, resting against the upright bed, a look of slight contentment spread across his face upon hearing that.

"Uncle Daniel, can I show you a picture of my family?" Magnus asked, pulling out his phone and scrolling to show Daniel a picture of all of them smiling together.

"Let's see. One, two, three kids. Wow. Almost on the way to your very own football team," Daniel laughed, looking at the picture closely with a smile.

"That's right. Two boys and a girl, and that is my wife, Erla. Been married fifteen years," Magnus told him.

"Oh, yes, if I recall correctly, I was there."

"No, you weren't. Aunt Doris was," Magnus corrected him awkwardly. "I don't know of any other way to say this. I always wanted to get to know you better. You are my only uncle."

"That is something very complicated," Daniel said, looking away, not wanting to meet his eye.

"Yeah, that is the same word my parents have used," Magnus replied, rolling his eyes and sighing in frustration. He was sick of hearing that word gloss over everything that happened between Pastor Jon and Daniel. "Can I at least get your side of the story? Maybe I can figure something out. Do you really want to leave this unresolved forever? I know my father wants it resolved. He really does."

"Again, Magnus, it's not easy, and I am sure he as well would not want you mixed up with the difficulties of that," Daniel said.

At that moment, there was a knock at the door, followed by the nurse walking into the room.

"Mr. Pallson, I am sorry to interrupt, but Doctor Walsh is here to check on you, and he does not have a lot of time to wait," she said apologetically, looking from the serious expression on Magnus's face to Daniel's.

"Can he wait a bit?" Daniel asked, hopefully.

"No, not tonight, I am afraid. He has surgery later," she replied.

"Oh, that is okay, I am running late myself. I've got to fly back to London," Magnus said, standing up as he did, still holding on to the picture of him and Thomas.

"Oh, you are leaving right now?" Daniel said, sitting up again to face Magnus.

"Yes, I hope to see you again soon, Uncle. Will you please consider what we talked about?"

"Good luck to you and your family, Magnus. Three kids and a nice wife. That is great. I will say I really appreciate your concern," answered Daniel, again shifting his gaze.

"I was hoping for more than that."

"Good night, Magnus," Daniel said, signaling the end of the conversation. Magnus wiped a small tear away as he left the room. He knew it would be hard to talk to his uncle, impossible even. But seeing him after all these years, coupled with the fact that it was his uncle who wanted to see him, Magnus really hoped they could have a heart-to-heart about what really mattered. It was apparent to Magnus what a hard time his uncle was going through, especially as he was still grappling with the loss of Thomas. Still, for some reason, Magnus thought that emotional vulnerability would lead to some resolution or reconciliation between the two brothers.

When Daniel dismissed him at the end of their conversation, it hit him much harder than he realized as he struggled to hold back tears once he was out of the room.

CHAPTER 9
LOOKING FOR WHAT IS LOST

The farm exuded an ethereal charm as the moonlight caressed the land with its silvery glow. It was quiet and serene, a haven of tranquility under the watchful gaze of the starlit sky. A gentle breeze whispered through the trees, carrying with it the scent of earth and wildflowers as if nature herself was exhaling a lullaby.

The moon, hanging high above the horizon, cast its radiant light upon the fields, illuminating the landscape in a soft, shimmering glow. The once-vibrant green meadows were now bathed in a pale, otherworldly hue, turning the familiar into something mystical and enchanting. The long grass swayed gracefully in the breeze, creating a symphony of whispers, as if the earth itself was engaged in a quiet conversation.

The farmhouse stood stoically, its walls weathered by time, and the elements combined with the modern, chic revamp done by Anna blended harmoniously with the surrounding landscape. Its windows were like portals to another realm, creating a cozy, inviting atmosphere. All appeared to be asleep, wrapped in the embrace of dreams, as the night held them in its delicate embrace.

In the distance, a stream meandered through the countryside, its gentle murmur accentuated by the nocturnal stillness. The water shimmered under the moon's radiant touch, like liquid silver flowing through the land. It seemed as though the stream was telling a story, recounting tales of faraway lands and ancient wisdom, a secret language only the night could decipher.

The silence was occasionally broken by the hushed rustling of leaves as nocturnal creatures ventured forth, exploring the nighttime wonders. A lone owl perched on a branch, its wise eyes gleaming in the moonlight and its haunting call punctuating the stillness with an otherworldly melody. The farm animals too rested peacefully, their contented sighs carrying on the wind.

As the night wore on, the sky became a masterpiece of celestial beauty. Countless stars adorned the heavens, twinkling like precious gems strewn across a vast canvas. The Milky Way, a cosmic river of stardust, arched across the sky, its celestial glow a testament to the wonders of the universe. It seemed as though one could reach out and pluck a star from the sky, cradling its brilliance in the palm of their hand.

In this tranquil oasis, time seemed to stand still, as if the world itself was holding its breath. Under the moonlit sky, the farm in Iceland was a sanctuary of peace and harmony, a testament to the awe-inspiring beauty of the natural world, until there was a knock at Pastor Jon and Anna's bedroom door. First softy and then louder. Daniel's night nurse was at the door.

"What happened?" asked Pastor Jon, the sleepiness in him completely vanishing as he was jolted alert seeing the panic on the nurse's face.

"It's about Mr. Pallson. He is missing. I can't find him anywhere!"

"Oh my goodness," gasped Anna from the back as Pastor Jon told the nurse they would be right out and meet her downstairs in a minute. They quickly dressed and made their way to the open space a floor below.

"I just went in to check how he was sleeping. He must have gone out the bedroom patio screen door," the nurse said when she saw them.

"How long since you last saw him?" asked Jon.

"When he went to bed about two hours ago," answered the nurse.

"Get Mr. Simon up too. I'll call the police and fire departments," Jon said firmly as Anna began dialing the numbers.

The moonlit night took on a sinister edge as Jon's heart raced with worry. The news of his brother Daniel's disappearance sent his mind racing. With each step, a sense of urgency propelled him toward Daniel's bedroom, hoping to uncover any clues that could lead him to Daniel's whereabouts.

As Jon entered the room, concern washed over him. The bed was unmade, the sheets in a mess, but there was no sign of Daniel. His eyes scanned the room, searching for any trace of his brother's presence. A sense of unease settled in as he noticed the scattered papers on the desk, an open financial book with a bookmark in the middle—evidence of Daniel's recent activities.

With cautious determination, Jon moved toward the screened patio, his steps echoing in the silence. The night air was crisp against his skin as he pushed open the door, revealing the landscape beyond. The moonlight spilled onto the ground, casting elongated shadows that danced with the gentle sway of the nearby trees. Taking a deep breath, he ventured outside, his eyes scanning the surroundings for any signs of Daniel's whereabouts.

His gaze fell upon the familiar spot where the golf cart usually resided. His heart sank as he realized it was missing. The absence of the vehicle deepened his concern, stirring a whirlwind of thoughts and questions in his mind. Why would Daniel take the golf cart in the middle of the night? Was he disoriented? Where could he have gone?

With each passing yard, Jon's mind raced, conjuring countless possibilities. Had Daniel wandered off aimlessly, lost in the vastness of the surrounding countryside? Or was there a purpose to his departure? The uncertainty gnawed at Jon's resolve, but he pushed forward, propelled by fear.

"The cart is gone. He took the damn cart," Jon said to Anna and Mr. Simon as they joined him on the patio.

The night air crackled with anticipation as the distant hum of a helicopter grew steadily louder, cutting through the tranquil stillness. Jon's eyes widened with hope as he raised his hand high above his head, waving fervently for the approaching aircraft to land directly in his vicinity.

The helicopter descended from the star-studded sky, its sleek silhouette outlined against the backdrop of moonlight. The rotating blades sliced through the air with a purposeful rhythm, producing a deep, resonant sound that reverberated through the surrounding landscape. It commanded attention, a beacon of assistance in the dark of night. As it neared the designated landing spot, the helicopter's impressive maneuverability became evident. The pilot guided the aircraft with precision, adjusting the pitch and angle of the blades to achieve a seamless descent. The helicopter's body glimmered in the moonlight, its metallic surface reflecting the ethereal glow, while its powerful presence seemed to command the air around it.

The helicopter settled onto the ground with a gentle touchdown, barely stirring the surrounding foliage. The landing was a symphony of coordinated movement—rotors slowing, engine power diminishing, and landing gear absorbing the weight. The abrupt cessation of the rotor's symphony brought a temporary stillness to the air.

As the dust settled, the helicopter stood like a sentinel before the sheriff walked out.

"Sheriff, thank you so much for all the help," Jon said, extending a hand toward him.

"Of course, Pastor. Glad to help. We'll find him," the sheriff told him reassuringly.

"It looks like he took the golf cart to wherever he went. The charge lasts up to four hours, but nobody remembers for sure how much of a charge it had when he took it."

"Okay. That means he could have gone almost anywhere. The nights this week have been colder than usual, so hopefully we'll find him soon. You grew up here and are well aware of the coyotes," the sheriff said, looking around the property.

"Of course, and Daniel, growing up here, knows that pretty well too. Come, let's go inside. I will show you the map of the ranch," Pastor Jon told him, pointing toward the patio. They went inside, and after greeting Anna and Mr. Simon, Jon showed him the map.

"If he were younger, I would tell you he knows this property and area like nobody else, but being older now and just surviving a heart attack, I don't think so anymore," Jon sighed.

At that moment, seven more men showed up in two different squad cars led by Deputy Norris.

"Sheriff, we got here as soon as we could," the deputy told him.

"Thanks for getting over here so quickly. Deputy Norris, this is Pastor Jon Pallson, brother of the missing Daniel Pallson."

Pastor Jon and Deputy Norris shook hands before a new chopper arrived to take Jon and the sheriff to look out. The helicopter's rotor blades sliced through the air as Pastor Jon and the sheriff sat side by side, their faces etched with determination. This new helicopter, arranged specifically for the search, surged forward with a renewed sense of purpose. Onboard, a team of officials diligently scanned the terrain below, their eyes peeled for any signs of Daniel.

As they flew over the farm, the pilot's voice crackled over the intercom, relaying vital information. "We have received an update," the pilot announced, his voice steady and composed. "Another patrol helicopter has spotted the missing golf cart approximately half a mile west of gate three."

A surge of hope coursed through Jon's veins, and he exchanged a brief glance with the sheriff, their eyes conveying a shared understanding. The search was intensifying, and the discovery of the golf cart brought them one step closer to finding Daniel. The helicopter veered toward the reported location with an accelerated speed, propelled by an urgent determination to reach the site swiftly. Ten minutes felt like an eternity as they covered the distance, each passing moment filled with anticipation and a touch of apprehension.

As they approached the designated area, Jon's heart raced with a mix of anticipation and trepidation. The landscape below came into view, and the sight of the golf cart nestled amidst the terrain sent a jolt of emotion through him. It was both a relief and a reminder of the challenges ahead.

The helicopter descended gracefully, landing near the golf cart, its blades slowing to a halt. The officials onboard quickly disembarked, fanning out to secure the area and examine the surroundings for any possible clues. Their presence was marked by a focused efficiency, with each member of the team diligently carrying out their assigned tasks.

Jon stepped out of the helicopter, his gaze fixed on the abandoned golf cart. It sat silently as if holding the secrets of Daniel's disappearance. He approached it cautiously, his heart pounding in his chest. As the team scoured the vicinity, a glimmer of hope emerged. A set of footprints, barely discernible amidst the uneven ground, caught the keen eyes of one of the officials. The discovery sparked renewed determination, igniting a fresh wave of energy in their search efforts.

"I think I see something blue, possibly a robe, moving on the ground. Like the description. From what I'm guessing, it looks like it is next to a graveyard." Dispatch told one of the officials with them.

"We will be right there," said the sheriff.

The family graveyard, nestled within the bounds of the farm, was silent and dark under the moonlit sky. The stillness of the night enveloped the area. As the search party approached the graveyard, their collective breaths held in anticipation. The darkness seemed to intensify, but they were not deterred. Flashlights and other illumination devices were swiftly produced, scattering beams of light across the somber landscape. The darkness retreated, unveiling the rows of gravestones that stretched out before them.

With each click of a flashlight switch, the graveyard transformed into an illuminated tableau. The soft glow illuminated the names and dates etched into the stone, revealing the legacies left behind by generations of the family. The play of light and shadow danced among the gravestones, casting an ethereal aura over the hallowed ground.

The search party moved cautiously, their footsteps hushed as they weaved through the maze of graves. The beams of light pierced the darkness, creating a patchwork of illumination that brought the graveyard to life. Whispers of the wind rustled through the leaves of nearby trees.

And then, amidst the solemnity, a gasp broke the silence. The beams of light converged on a figure sprawled face down on one of the graves. Time seemed to stand still as the search party's eyes widened in disbelief. The body was motionless, its presence an enigma that defied explanation.

As the search party cautiously approached, their flashlights trained on the fallen form, and a mix of emotions swirled within them. With the weight of uncertainty hanging heavy in the air, whispers of concern and hushed exclamations filled the night, echoing off the gravestones.

In the glow of the flashlights, the search party, led by the sheriff, rushed to Daniel's body to see if he was still breathing or not.

CHAPTER 10
CATCH AND RELEASE

As the search party approached the family graveyard, a sense of unease hung in the air. The tension thickened with each step closer to the solemn site. Daniel was covered in a layer of dirt that clung to his body from head to toe, marring his features and obscuring his identity.

The sheriff and Pastor Jon were the first to reach him. Daniel was alive, but his state of being was far from coherent. His disheveled appearance, coupled with the mud-caked robe he wore, only added to the mystery surrounding his circumstances.

As they drew closer, the harsh reality of the situation became apparent. Daniel's face bore a haunting expression of confusion and disarray. His hair, usually neatly groomed, now clung in wild tangles, matted with the earth that clung to his body. His eyes seemed distant and unfocused, a reflection of the turmoil within his mind. They darted aimlessly, unable to settle on a single point of focus, as if he were struggling to comprehend his surroundings. His breathing was labored.

Gently, the sheriff and Pastor Jon approached, their concern etched deeply into their faces. They exchanged glances, silently acknowledging the seriousness of the situation. With utmost care, they reached out to Daniel, helping him onto his side to assess his condition. Questions flooded their minds, but they knew that immediate medical attention was the first priority.

"Get those paramedics here now!" the sheriff called as Daniel mumbled a string of incomprehensible words under his breath.

"Will, what are you saying?" said Pastor Jon gently.

Daniel continued to grumble something.

"You what? You had to do what?" asked Pastor Jon softly, putting his ear to Daniel's lips.

"Talk to Thomas." Pastor Jon could barely make it out.

"He said to talk to his late son Thomas, whose grave he was lying on," Pastor Jon explained as the paramedics arrived and came to check his vitals.

"All his vitals look good. We should get him cleaned up and back to his bed. I have confirmed with his doctor that he will be arriving shortly," a paramedic told them decisively before Pastor Jon thanked all those who had come out to search, and they headed back to the farm.

Back in the comfort of Daniel's room, two diligent nurses set to work, determined to clean him up and restore a sense of normalcy. The room was softly lit, casting a warm and soothing glow upon the scene.

The first nurse approached with a gentle smile, radiating compassion and care. She carried a basin filled with warm water and a stack of soft towels. The second nurse followed closely behind, her eyes holding a reassuring demeanor. The first nurse moistened a towel in the basin, wringing out the excess water before carefully dabbing at the layers of mud that clung stubbornly to Daniel's weary body. She worked methodically, being mindful of his fragile state. With each stroke of the towel, the layers of dirt began to give way, revealing glimpses of the man underneath.

The second nurse stood nearby, holding a soft robe in her hands, ready to clothe Daniel once he was cleansed. Her soothing presence provided a sense of comfort amidst the otherwise chaotic situation. As she continued to cleanse his face, neck, and arms, the other nurse gently guided Daniel's legs into a basin of warm water, soothing his aching muscles and relieving the weight of the muddy residue.

The nurses worked in harmony, their movements synchronized and purposeful. They approached their task with unwavering professionalism, yet their compassion shone through every action. As they tended to Daniel's physical needs, they offered gentle words of encouragement, assuring him that he was safe and cared for. Once Daniel was thoroughly cleansed, they carefully helped him back into bed. Jon and Doris were waiting anxiously nearby, concern etched onto their faces. The room felt serene, a sanctuary amidst the storm that had engulfed their lives.

As Daniel settled into the comfort of his bed, supported by soft pillows and warm blankets, he found solace in the familiar presence of Jon and Doris. Their eyes met, filled with unspoken relief. The room exuded a sense of quiet strength as the nurses silently withdrew, leaving the family with some privacy before the doctor arrived.

"I talked to Thomas," Daniel told Doris as she held onto his hands.

"I'm sure he loved hearing from you," she told him, her voice heavy with emotion.

"I could have done more. We could have done more," Daniel said, turning his face away from her to look at Jon. "Jon, I want you to know I am so happy for Magnus becoming such a great young man, but when I see him, I can't help but think about Thomas at the same age and how great he would have been too. That's why I have avoided Magnus all these years."

"Come on, Daniel, just concentrate on getting some rest for now, okay?" Jon told him, soothingly touching his arm.

In the sanctuary of his bed, emotions welled up within Daniel, threatening to consume him. Jon looked at him, his own eyes filled with a mixture of empathy and sorrow, knowing the depth of his brother's pain. The room seemed to hold its breath as if acknowledging the weight of their conversation. As Daniel's voice quivered, his words trembled with grief, bearing the raw wounds of loss. Tears cascaded down his cheeks, each drop a testament to the love he held for his departed son. His voice cracked with anguish, punctuated by moments of choked silence, as he struggled to articulate the depths of his sorrow.

"I miss him, Jon," Daniel choked out, his voice barely a whisper. "Every day, it's like a piece of me is missing. I think about him, and it's like an ache that won't go away. I should have done more. I should have been there for him. How could I have let this happen?"

His voice trailed off, consumed by the weight of regret. Jon listened, his heart heavy with understanding, aware that no words could truly alleviate the pain his brother must be feeling. The room held an air of profound sadness as if it was mourning alongside them.

Daniel's grief was a vast ocean, engulfing him in its turbulent waves. He grappled with the haunting thoughts of what could have been, his mind replaying moments of missed opportunities and questioning his role as a parent. The weight of responsibility pressed upon him, amplifying the ache of loss.

Jon reached out, his touch a tender gesture of solace. No words were exchanged, for none could truly heal the wounds that Daniel carried within. Instead, they sat in sacred silence, allowing the pain to exist, acknowledging the complexity of grief and the vastness of love.

As the room embraced their shared sorrow, Daniel's voice softened, his sobs quieting to gentle whispers.

"I'm honestly envious of you and Anna. You did such a great job with Magnus," Daniel said after the silence.

"You shouldn't feel that way. You and Doris did all you could for Thomas," Jon reassured him while Doris broke out into soft, contained sobs.

"I know I should have done better. Tough love, things that could have saved him."

"Well, you know what I say," Jon began, to which he and Daniel said, "It's God's plan," in unison as Doris's cries became louder.

"Please, no more of that 'it's God's plan' stuff between the two of you," Daniel said to Jon and Doris.

"How dare you?" Doris managed to get out before she turned to leave the room, still crying.

"Come on, I didn't mean it that way," Daniel called out to her to no avail.

"How could you say that?" said Jon, visibly upset by Daniel's comment. "Get some rest," he said before leaving the room himself to console Doris.

Jon hurried after her, a mix of concern and determination on his face, leaving behind the heaviness that lingered in the room.

Finding Doris in the hallway, Pastor Jon approached her with gentle steps, aware of the delicate nature of her emotions. His eyes reflected a deep understanding of her pain, and his voice carried a soothing tone as he reached out to console her.

"Doris," he said softly, his voice filled with empathy, "I understand how hurtful those words were. Daniel is going through immense pain, and his grief is causing him to lash out. It's not easy for any of us." Tears continued to fall down Doris's cheeks as she looked into Jon's compassionate eyes. She was grappling with her own sorrow, her heart burdened by the loss of their son and the complicated dynamics that had unfolded over the years. Jon, knowing the weight of her emotions, extended a comforting hand, gently placing it on her trembling shoulder. It was a gesture of solace and support, an attempt to bridge the emotional distance between them.

"I know it's hard to hear, but Daniel is hurting. His anger and disbelief are part of his grief journey," he continued, his voice a steady presence in the midst of her turmoil. "We can't change what happened, but we can find strength in each other."

Doris clung to those words, finding a glimmer of solace in Jon's compassionate wisdom. She leaned into his touch, finding a small measure of comfort in his presence. His empathy offered a lifeline amidst the turbulent sea of emotions she was navigating. It always had. He and Anna had been true family to her despite her relationship with Daniel, and she valued them now more than ever.

Together, they stood in that hallway, enveloped in the sorrow that had shaped their lives. Pastor Jon offered Doris a safe space to grieve, to release her pain, and to acknowledge the complexity of their shared loss. He became a source of solace in his quiet strength and understanding, allowing her tears to flow and reminding her that she was not alone in her suffering. With a gentle squeeze of her shoulder, Pastor Jon conveyed his unwavering support and offered Doris the space she needed to process her emotions. In that moment, the hallway became a sanctuary of shared grief and understanding.

Back in Daniel's room, Doctor Walsh had just entered and was looking over Daniel's chart with the latest readings of his vitals.

"Took an unplanned walk, huh?" the doctor asked him as Daniel's face was still a little red and swollen from the tears he had shed.

"Something like that," Daniel murmured, looking away from him.

"Good news is all vitals are stable. It could have been a really bad situation for many reasons, you understand that? It looks like you can still go back home on schedule, but I still want the nurse to go with us."

"Okay. We are going back on my plane, right?" Daniel confirmed, sitting up a bit on the bed as the doctor's pager went off.

"That's the plan, and the arrangements have already been made. Okay, I will see you tomorrow. And remember, rest!" ordered Doctor Walsh while looking at his pager and walking out the door. Daniel felt a mixture of relief and trepidation wash over him. The prospect of resuming his life seemed daunting, for he knew that the road ahead was fraught with challenges.

Alone in his room, Daniel got up from his bed and settled into a chair, his gaze drifting toward the window, lost in the depths of his thoughts. His heart weighed heavy with grief. The prospect of moving forward seemed inconceivable when he felt so entangled in the tendrils of his past over the last few days.

Contemplation enveloped him as he grappled with the work he knew he had to do. The resort, the reporters, the company. In the stillness of that moment, Daniel acknowledged that the future held uncertainties, yet he also recognized the spark of resilience within himself.

CHAPTER 11
THE CURRENT OF MEMORIES

As the golden rays of the morning sun gently kissed the Icelandic morning, Pastor Jon and Doris sat at the kitchen table, savoring their steaming cups of coffee and indulging in the splendor unfolding before their eyes as if to distract themselves from the emotions they were feeling.

The light danced upon the lush green fields, painting a striking tapestry of colors across the landscape. Dewdrops glistened like scattered diamonds on the vibrant blades of grass, while delicate wildflowers in hues of purple, yellow, and white swayed gracefully in the gentle breeze that made its way through the open window in front of the kitchen, which was nearly ceiling to wall to allow for a broad view.

There was a symphony of nature awakening around them. A chorus of birds sang melodies of joy, their sweet notes intertwining with the distant sound of grazing horses and the gentle babbling of a nearby stream.

"He never admitted to me that was why he seemed to avoid Magnus, but I pretty much knew that. I always felt sorry for Magnus because of it," Doris said after a while, finally breaking the silence once her coffee was almost finished.

"One time, not long ago, Magnus mentioned he felt like that might be true, and I told him if it was, it was obviously in no way his fault," Jon replied reassuringly, sensing the remorse in her voice.

"Did you ever know that sometimes, until when Thomas got into trouble, Daniel would go to church with us? I will never forget that one day after Thomas was born, he told me there were too many beautiful things in the world not to consider being a believer in something bigger. Sometimes, he even prayed with me after we found out Thomas was involved in drugs, but when Thomas passed, he said he wanted nothing to do with religion or spirituality ever again, as it just lets him down," Doris continued.

"That was the time Daniel shut me out. And being a pastor of a church must have made it even more difficult for him to be with me." There was a hint of realization in Jon's tone as he told her that. He let out a heavy sigh before shaking his head.

"So, you noticed this soon after Thomas's death and before your dispute with the family land, which was what, five years after?" Doris asked him, standing up to wash her empty coffee mug and put it away.

"Definitely. I think he seemed to have less respect toward me and possibly made it easier to butt heads with me over the estate, knowing I would be upset," Jon admitted as she solemnly agreed.

A few hours later, Reverend Adams was packed and ready to leave. Doris and Adams shared a tender embrace, their bond palpable to those around them.

Awaiting her departure, an SUV stood by, its engine humming softly. Jon and Anna both hugged her goodbye before Jon helped her put her suitcase in the trunk, and Dagur waved from beside them.

As the SUV began its slow retreat, the entrance door swung open, and Daniel came out to the edge of the door using a walker. Deep wrinkles, once subtle, now carved intricate patterns across his features, speaking of the weight of his experiences, etching a somber expression on his face. Dressed in jeans and a wrinkled shirt that seemed unwearable, a stark contrast to the impeccably tailored suits that once adorned his form. A man reduced to a mere shadow of the commanding business mogul he had been just a few weeks ago.

Behind the walker, Daniel seemed smaller. His eyes, once sharp and clear, now appeared weary as the fire that once burned brightly within him seemed dimmed, replaced by a quiet resignation. The vibrant colors of the farm, the sun's warm embrace, and the gentle breeze passing through the fields seemed distant and detached, almost as if they were passing through him as well.

"Good morning," Pastor Jon said as Daniel worked his way to where they were standing.

"Yes, indeed, this is a good morning." Lowering his voice, he added, "We finally got rid of her?" Daniel remarked in Jon's ear.

"Daniel, come on now, especially not in front of the kid," Jon scolded, gesturing toward Dagur.

* * *

As Daniel tossed and turned in bed, his mind took him back to a time from long ago.

There was a fishing river nestled within the captivating landscape of the farm. There, on the banks of this natural marvel, Daniel found himself accompanied by Thomas, aged ten, and Magnus, aged eleven at the time.

The river currents, which were swift and purposeful, flowed with a melodic rhythm, whispering secrets to the stones that lined its bed. Silver ribbons of water weaved through the emerald tapestry, their shimmering dance an invitation to partake in their mysterious depths. Veils of mist danced delicately above the river's surface, lending an ethereal aura to the scene.

The air was crisp and fragrant, carrying the scent of damp earth and moss. The gentle breeze whispered through the gnarled branches of the nearby trees as if sharing the secrets of centuries past. The foliage, a tapestry of vibrant greens, dappled the landscape with shades of life and growth. Dragonflies, like shimmering jewels, hovered above the water's surface, their delicate wings reflecting the sun's radiance.

Against this backdrop of nature's grandeur, they stood in harmony with the river's timeless rhythm, laughing and talking amongst themselves.

"Tommy, I think I got him!" Daniel exclaimed, wrestling with his fishing rod.

"Dad, careful, don't lose it!" Thomas said, wading over to his father.

"Is it a big one?" called out Magnus from a slight distance with a massive grin slapped across his face as he squinted, trying to make out the size of the fish at the end of Daniel's hook. Daniel grappled with the fish with all his strength as Thomas helped his father. He handed Thomas the control of the fishing rod as the battle raged on.

"It's the oldest and most famous fish ever in this lake. His name is Godzilla, as he's the biggest ever seen. I have been after fish for years. This time, we got him!" Daniel stated over the splashing of the water.

"We've got to let the line out a bit, and then we bring her back in. Here it comes!" Thomas responded gleefully.

"Yes, Son, there you go. You got it."

As Thomas reeled in the fish, a mixture of excitement and anticipation coursed through his veins. The fish, sensing its impending capture, fought back with relentless vigor, desperate to reclaim its freedom. The tension mounted as the line strained under the weight of the struggle. Time seemed to slow as Thomas fought against the powerful resistance. Each second felt like an eternity, his muscles taut with determination. The surface of the water shimmered with expectancy as if holding its breath, waiting for the climax of this duel.

But fate, in its whimsy, intervened. In an abrupt twist, the line snapped, setting the fish free. A collective gasp escaped from Thomas, Daniel, and Magnus's lips, mingling with the soft sigh of the wind. The fish, triumphant in its escape, vanished into the depths, leaving only ripples as a bittersweet testament to its fleeting presence.

Thomas stood there, his gaze fixed upon the spot where the elusive adversary had disappeared. A mixture of disappointment and embarrassment welled up inside him.

"Oh damn. Not again," cursed Daniel as Thomas turned to look at him.

"I'm so sorry, Dad. I screwed it up."

"You didn't screw it up. I've told you about this fish so many times. It always gets away from me, no matter how hard I try. You didn't screw up, Son!" Daniel told him fiercely, walking over to put his hands on his son's shoulders.

"No, Dad, I did, as I always do."

"Stop that nonsense. That was never true. Why can't you stop doing that to yourself?" Daniel questioned, a strained urgency in his tone.

"When are you going to quit blaming yourself…and Mom? I was old enough to know better. Those things just happened. I got caught up with the wrong crowd. It's life. I tried. I really did," Thomas argued, clearly meaning more than the lost fish.

"I know you tried, Son. I know you did," said Daniel, nodding.

"You know, Magnus was right about that photograph. We had a lot of happy times before I got into trouble," Thomas told him. "I gotta go now, Dad. I love you, and tell Mom I will always love her too. I have faith in you, Dad, just like you always had faith in me."

"Son, don't leave, not yet," Daniel implored, his voice trembling as he did.

"I hope to see ya again, Dad, but that's up to you," declared Thomas in the most serious and straightforward way possible.

Daniel stirred from his afternoon slumber, his mind still entangled in the dream. The remnants of a recurring vision lingered in his consciousness, elusive yet familiar. A perplexing mixture of intrigue and disquiet settled upon him as he shifted his gaze toward the ceiling, his thoughts filled with Thomas and the river.

In the vast expanse of his emotions, waves of anguish crashed against the shores of his being. Each breath carried the weight of a thousand unspoken words. A symphony of pain flooded his senses as he curled into the fetal position and began to cry. This was a dream he had had many times before, and he woke up with the same crippling agony each time. The tendrils of grief wound tightly around his shattered heart, an unyielding grip that refused to release him from its melancholic embrace.

Memories, both tender and haunting, troubled the corridors of his mind, threading a tapestry of bittersweet remembrance. In the solitude of the afternoon, Daniel sought solace amidst the fragments of a shattered existence. The ache of absence reverberated through his being, a void that could never be filled no matter how many acquisitions or mergers he made, yet he was not ready to accept the profoundness of that particular truth.

Awareness cascaded through his awakening mind, nudging him to action. Daniel yearned for answers, for a glimpse beyond the ephemeral curtain that separated dreams from reality. With a solemn gaze, he reached out to the bedside phone to summon the nurse.

CHAPTER 12
THE DREAM

THE SUN HUNG low in the evening sky, casting a fiery glow upon the vast expanse of the Pallson ranch. Daniel stared fixedly at the vivid and incandescent colors that graced the wide horizon. Iceland indeed had the most beautiful skies. The whole scene looked surreal and somewhat illusory to Daniel, as all the time he spent working in bustling cities surrounded by urbane architecture had made him overlook the simple and immaculate beauty of raw and unscathed nature.

As Daniel lounged upon a comfortable chair on the patio outside his room, he admired the dazzling landscape blessing his eyes. The absence of malevolent smoke and loud traffic from the atmosphere was a welcome addition. The air was clean and fresh. A cool and calming breeze brushed Daniel's face every now and then. He spread his legs in front of him, relaxing his back. He had long given up reading the book about the new and enhanced tips on mindful and rewarding stock market investments. But even as he peered upon the extraordinary view in front of him, his thoughts were completely consumed and preoccupied with the remainder of his recurring dream. It was all he could think about.

The young face of his son and the words he said to him in the dream flashed across his mind. What did Thomas mean? What did he intend when he said that he hoped to meet Daniel again? Thomas was dead. The thought sent shivers down Daniel's spine, but it was the truth. He was never meeting his son again. And although he hadn't made peace with the fact, he wasn't foolish enough to hope for the contrary.

While Daniel was a practical man who did not believe in anything supernatural or metaphysical, he was very curious about dreams—a way through which the subconscious probably interacted with and alerted the conscious mind. Therefore, he sometimes attempted to interpret dreams he had in order to prepare for any threats or turbulences in his possible future. Daniel also knew that this recurring dream was perhaps the most powerful and mind-boggling one he had ever had. He was, therefore, trying extra hard to understand its meaning. However, the whole process was unnerving and agitating. He was at a loss for any sort of viable explanation for the dream. How could it be in Daniel's hands to meet his son again? This was the part that troubled him the most. He knew for a fact that if there was even the slightest chance or a flickering possibility for him to see his son again, even for an infinitesimal moment, he would move the heavens and the earth for it. He would go to all lengths, disregarding all consequences. All his wealth, success, power, and fame were secondary to him. They held no importance and no significance compared to the love and the yearning he felt for his son. His only son, the light of his life, who was now resting six feet below the ground.

Daniel was lost in these deeply pensive thoughts when he heard the patio door open. Jon's face peeked outside. He smiled at Daniel when he spotted him.

"There you are! Mind if I join you?" Jon asked as he made himself comfortable on the sofa beside Daniel. He held a small brown envelope in one hand and a cup of tea in another.

Jon's arrival pulled Daniel out of his somber and disturbing thoughts.

"I had forgotten how beautiful this place was," Daniel mused.

Jon smiled again as he extended the envelope in Daniel's direction. Daniel looked at it for a second. Jon impatiently nudged it forward as Daniel took it from him. He opened the envelope and realized that there were pictures inside of it. He took them out and started looking through them. The photographs were of Jon and Daniel's childhood and their parents. They were all so happy and young.

"I had a copy made for you," Jon told Daniel.

"Thank you!" Daniel replied while still staring at the pictures. "Wow, it's amazing how sometimes these days feel like yesterday and other times like forever ago," he added.

He looked through the pictures for a few more minutes, completely engrossed in them. The whole time, Jon gazed at him while sipping his tea. He noticed the smile that graced Daniel's face whenever he came across an especially merry picture. He noticed that even though Daniel wasn't in the best of health, there were significantly fewer lines smeared across his forehead, and his entire demeanor was less rigid and more relaxed than it had been in years.

As Daniel stared at a family picture of a childhood fishing trip, he chuckled involuntarily. Jon leaned it to look at it. In the photograph, Jon was standing by the side of the river with a big boot in his hand, which he had caught instead of a fish.

Jon smiled at his brother's amusement.

"The clean air has been good for you," he commented.

Daniel looked at Jon as he placed the pictures on the oakwood table in front of him. He sighed, sitting straighter in his chair.

"So, still want to talk about the river?" Daniel said.

"No, not anymore. That issue is closed now. All I want now is to see you get completely well as soon as possible," Jon told him.

"Really?" Daniel asked.

"Yes, really. But there is one thing I wanted to talk about."

"Oh no, whenever you say that, it's never good," Daniel sighed.

"It's about Doris," Jon replied.

"Like I said, it's never good. What have I done to displease you now, little brother?" said Daniel.

"I don't like the way you treat her, Dan," Jon said calmly.

Even though Jon's tone was soft and polite, Daniel took offense to his statement.

"These are dangerous grounds, Jon. You better tread carefully," he warned.

However, Jon understood the importance of having this conversation. He knew that he needed to talk some sense into his brother. He was already prepared for all sorts of retaliation, so he continued.

"Do you not see how much she's done for you? The sacrifices she has made. She flew all the way to Iceland for you, even though she had no obligation whatsoever. You have no right to treat her the way you do, especially when she has done nothing wrong," Jon said.

This struck a nerve with Daniel as anger and frustration tainted his features. He was infuriated, and it was evident in his expressions. How could Jon blame Daniel for his broken relationship with Doris when it was never his fault?

"Done nothing wrong? She left me, damn it! It wasn't me who walked out. She is the one responsible for our wrecked relationship, not me!" Daniel fumed.

"It was you. Just like you shut me out of your life, you did the same to her," Jon said, trying to make Daniel understand.

"How dare you? How can you—""Tell me it isn't true!" Jon said. "Tell me you didn't ignore and disregard her just like you did me."

Daniel wanted to reply but chose to stay silent. He didn't want to fight with his brother. He had no energy and no intention to do so. He leaned back in his chair once again.

Jon continued in a calmer tone, "Daniel, you had a heart attack. It's a miracle that you are alive. God knows how long you have left. It is time to address and acknowledge the things that have been eating you up on the inside for so long. If you can just try to forgive yourself for what happened, you might move on."

"Easy for you to say. You didn't lose a son," Daniel scoffed.

"No, but I lost a brother! It's been over two decades now, and not only do you blame yourself, but you also blame me. I'm not saying that you're wrong to do so, because you aren't. It was my fault too. I thought that coming here to work in the summer would help with straightening Thomas out. I thought that the farm would keep him busy and maybe help him get better. I thought there were fewer ways to get into trouble here."

"Well, he sure as hell found one of those fewer ways here in the good old place of the midnight sun, didn't he?" taunted Daniel.

"Daniel, please understand. I had no idea that he was hanging out with that crowd. I didn't know they were selling him drugs. I was doing my best to help Thomas, and you know that. How many times will I have to apologize for you to finally forgive me?"

"You don't have to apologize anymore, Jon. I know that it wasn't your fault."

"Really? You mean that?"

"Yes."

"Well, you have an odd way of showing it."

"The truth is, I never should've blamed you. The weight of my son's death lies with me. Not you. Not Doris. Me. It's an unforgivable, unacceptable, and cruel truth, but the truth nonetheless." Daniel paused and took a deep breath.

"Thomas was the best thing that ever happened to me. He was my joy and my happiness. My life revolved around him; he was my axis. When he died, it felt as though my world had collapsed and time had stopped. Nothing was of consequence anymore. Everything was useless and mundane, unnecessary and irrelevant. I couldn't move on, and the more Doris went to church or therapy, the worse it became for me. She was accepting his death, coming to terms with it, and just that thought alone was unbearable for me."

"She was dealing with the loss in her own way, Daniel. You can't blame her for it," Jon said.

"I knew that. I just think that she moved on from losing Thomas too quickly."

"Doris has never forgotten Thomas. You know that, Daniel! You have to understand that we all grieve differently. There is no right or wrong and no too fast or too quickly. Doris just learned how to handle her pain," Jon explained.

This angered Daniel. His tone became rather harsh as he said, "What do you want me to say, Jon? Unlike many others, I couldn't shake the pain of my son's death, and it really sucks! Do you want me to apologize for grieving? Should I be sorry for wanting some closure, some explanation? Is that what you're after?"

"Not at all," said Jon quickly. "You are taking my words the wrong way. I know that you're in immeasurable pain, and I understand that pain like this never really goes away. All I'm saying is that you have to stop beating yourself up about it. You need to forgive yourself and all others who you blame for what happened to Thomas. You're older now, Daniel. You don't have the strength to harbor all this anger inside of you. It almost killed you."

These words from Jon made Daniel realize that his brother was right. There was so much pain inside of him, overpowering and beyond endurance. He was broken and defeated, utterly disturbed. On top of that, he couldn't stop thinking about the dream he had. Thomas's words were etched inside his mind, torturing him. He wanted answers, and he wanted them now. He looked at his brother and realized that Jon might be the person who could help him in this situation. He was a pastor; it was quite literally his job. That was when Daniel decided to share his secret.

"I have been having these recurring dreams for years now," Daniel began.

"Are they about Thomas?" Jon inquired.

Daniel nodded as he replied, "It's always the same. I am fishing with Thomas and Magnus. They are around ten years old. Suddenly, I catch that salmon that is famous on the lake for being the biggest ever."

"You mean Godzilla?"

"Yes, that's the fish. Thomas comes to help me. We almost get the fish when it slips away. After that, Thomas starts blaming himself for the lost fish. He says that he always disappoints me. Then he tells me that we shouldn't feel guilty about him. It's the same dream over and over again."

After a moment of silence, Daniel asked Jon, "What do you think this means, Mister Man of God?"

Instead of answering right away, Jon began with some questions.

"Have you ever told Doris?" he asked, to which Daniel shook his head, indicating that he had never told Doris about his dream.

"When did it start?" Jon further inquired.

"It was shortly after Thomas died," Daniel answered.

"That's a long time," commented Jon.

"Some days, it feels like yesterday," sighed Daniel.

"Dreams are not easy to explain. Trying to make any definite conclusions is a very risky proposition. I have a few people in my parish who I have counseled about grief and the loss of loved ones. They admit to having dreams but not as long or repetitive as yours."

"I can't say that I am a religious person, but sometimes I wonder if Thomas is trying to get a message to me. Maybe he wants to tell me something."

"It could be—or maybe it's your own subconsciousness that's trying to communicate with you. God can show up in mysterious ways for anyone wanting His help. You just have to be willing enough to accept it," explained Jon.

"I just told you I'm not a religious man, Jon. I don't think God will help me."

"Just because you don't believe in Him doesn't mean God isn't there. Your disbelief does not disqualify you from receiving God's will and mercy."

Daniel didn't have a reply to that, and Jon stood up as he heard Dagur calling out for him.

"Better go check on Dagur," said Jon.

Daniel offered his right hand to shake with Jon as he was about to leave, but instead Jon bent down and gave Daniel a hug. Daniel was taken by surprise, and every part of his body tensed up. He froze from head to toe as if he had had some sort of an allergic reaction to affection. After a few awkward seconds, Jon let go and headed out of the room. However, before exiting, he turned and looked at Daniel.

"Get better, and I mean it."

Daniel, who was still confused and confounded by his brother's sudden show of intimacy, could only respond by asking, "Why did you do that?"

"I did that because you're my brother and because I love you! And if you really loved me, you would admit that I was actually a better athlete than you ever were."

"In your dreams," teased Daniel as Jon exited the patio with a smile.

CHAPTER 13
THE SURPRISE VISIT

IT WAS A clear and bright Sunday morning. The last day of the week was of great importance in the Pallson household, as the entire family visited the church to attend Jon's sermon. Jon had left the ranch early in the morning, clutching his best-loved copy of the Bible. He was dressed in a long black cassock and neat white surplice that fell to his knees. In addition to that, he had a matching black stole draped over his shoulders.

Anna, Doris, and Dagur left a little while later. They didn't ask Daniel to accompany them, as he had made his stance on all matters pertaining to religion and God entirely too clear. The route to the church wasn't long or time-consuming. After just a few minutes of trailing across the vast and expansive grass-covered plains, they could spot the church in the distance.

Jon's church was situated on a small hill overlooking an awe-inspiring valley. Its structure was old-fashioned and picturesque. The pearly-white exterior and the dark-red roof of the quaint building stood out against the lush green high ground. The side of the church was lined with a series of colorful kaleidoscopic windows that were sealed shut, keeping the mildly cold morning air at bay. Anna, Doris, and Dagur ascended the hill easily and made their way into the house of prayer. They entered through the tall wooden doors and walked across the numerous lines of wooden pews until they reached the front row, where they seated themselves.

The interior of the church was old but beautiful. The nave was spacious, while the oakwood altar was adorned with a huge Jesus mural. Sunlight filtering through the stained-glass windows cast an ethereal and luminous glow within the church. The atmosphere was serene and peaceful as churchgoers of all ages poured through the open doorway. Near the front of the church, beside the altar, children dressed in black choir gowns gathered. They took their places on the wooden seats allocated for them. As the congregants began to settle, the choir started singing. It was so sublimely melodious that even the visitors chanted and chimed.

After the choir finished singing, Jon took his place on the pulpit and began delivering his sermon.

"Thank you!" he said. "That is one of my favorite Psalms, so beautiful. Let us pray."

The churchgoers bowed their heads in prayer, and a tranquil silence spread across the room. However, at this very moment, the attention of all the people inside the church was drawn toward the big front doors that opened with a loud noise. Although the prayer continued, many churchgoers glanced back to eye the latecomers. The silhouettes of two men appeared in the doorway, and even though they attempted to talk in low whispers, their voices reverberated across the room in loud echoes. As the duo walked further into the room, their faces became clear. Jon was most shocked upon realizing who had entered the room, along with Anna and Doris, who were equally perplexed. It was Daniel and Mr. Simon.

"There are some seats over there. Let's move," Daniel instructed Mr. Simon in a hushed whisper.

"Yes, Mr. Pallson," Simon replied.

They started moving toward the empty seats that were situated at the end of a pew. A few people had to stand in order to let the two of them pass. Daniel was using a cane, which made this embarrassing journey even more difficult. He almost fell, trying to navigate his way, but Mr. Simon caught him before he hit the ground. When they finally reached the empty seats and managed to sit down, they smiled and apologized to the people next to them.

"You boys comfortable?" Jon asked with a little smile.

Some people snickered, and a few laughed after hearing this, including Daniel and Mr. Simon.

"Thank you!" Daniel told the young man sitting beside him.

"The old gray mare ain't what it used to be," he further remarked in a voice loud enough to be heard across the room.

The whole church erupted with laughter at this humorous comment, including Jon. He shook his head as he said, "Let's continue with our prayer, if it suits you, gentlemen."

Daniel waved his hand at Jon, motioning him to continue.

"Let us sing!" Jon announced, and so they did. Every person in the church started singing, led by the choir.

Daniel and Mr. Simon were the only ones who couldn't join, as their Icelandic was simply not good enough. However, they enjoyed the musical chants immensely.

Later on, Jon headed toward the front door, and most of the churchgoers followed suit while the choir carried on with their soulful melody. Daniel and Mr. Simon also started moving toward the exit. Jon paused on his way to the door and grabbed his brother's arm, supporting and leading him outdoors. The three men stopped near the top steps of the enchanting church.

"What a pleasant surprise seeing you here!" Jon told Daniel.

"I thought it was time I visited your office. Sorry, we were a little late," Daniel interjected with a smile.

"No problem, glad you could make it."

"You're good at this."

Coming from Daniel, this compliment meant a whole lot more to Jon than it normally would have. "Thank you. You should come more often," he told him.

"I just might," Daniel uttered without thinking. He realized what he had just said and decided that it was best to simply change the subject. "Did Doris come as well? I haven't seen her," he asked.

Jon smiled as he said, "I take it listening to the Word of God was not the main reason for your visit."

"Of course it was. Now, will you answer my question?" Daniel said impatiently.

Jon eyed his brother for a second before answering. "They were sitting in the front, should be out any minute."

He then directed his attention toward Mr. Simon, who was standing silently beside Daniel the whole time. He was dressed in a crisp blue suit, which seemed fancy and too formal for a church visit. In his hands was a beautiful bouquet of flowers, fresh pink tulips.

"Are the flowers for me, Mr. Simon?" Jon asked him.

"I'm afraid not," Mr. Simon answered.

While the three of them conversed with one another, the line to greet the Pastor grew. Jon realized that he needed to attend to the people lining up behind him.

"Why don't you go sit down? I will ask Doris and Anna to join us," he said to Daniel and Mr. Simon.

"Splendid idea," Daniel replied as he signaled Mr. Simon to come along.

The two of them made their way to the table and seated themselves.

A little while later, Doris and Anna stepped outside. Dagur was still inside, harmonizing with the choir. The two of them walked up to Jon, who was halfway through his meet-and-greet session.

"Is he still here?" Doris asked Jon.

"He's waiting for you!" Jon pointed toward the table where Daniel and Mr. Simon were seated.

"This man is killing me!" Doris exclaimed as she turned toward Anna. "Please come with me," she asked her.

Anna nodded as the two of them advanced in the direction of Daniel's table.

When the duo seated at the table noticed Doris and Anna walking toward them, Daniel stood up and pulled out a chair for Doris. Anna settled into the chair beside her.

"Here, sit down. Happy to see you both!" Daniel said. "How have you been?" he asked Doris.

"How have I been? You know how I have been, Daniel!"

"Not really."

The two of them looked at each other for a long moment as the choir serenaded the audience in the background.

Doris looked away and turned her attention toward Mr. Simon.

"Good afternoon, Mr. Simon!" she greeted him.

"Good afternoon, Doris and Anna."

"Good afternoon!" Anna chimed in.

Mr. Simon gave her a small smile before addressing Daniel.

"Please excuse me, Mr. Pallson. Can I speak to you for a second?" Simon interrupted.

"Sure," Daniel replied. He excused himself from Doris and Anna before he walked a few feet away from the table with Mr. Simon. They discussed something for a couple of seconds before Mr. Simon walked away. Daniel made his way back to the table, but instead of sitting down he marched straight up to Doris and whispered something into her ear. Jon had also joined the party by this time. Doris looked a little uncomfortable as Daniel continued whispering.

"It'd be rude to leave the table," she told Daniel after a few moments.

"Please come! It's completely okay."

"But…"

"No buts, come on, get up," Daniel insisted.

"Alright! Just for a few minutes," she caved.

"Please excuse us. We will be right back," Daniel announced to the other people at the table.

Even as she got out of her chair, Doris could not think of a single thing of consequence that Daniel might want to discuss. She had no idea why he was pulling her away from the rest of the family. Be that as it may, Doris knew that Daniel was a practical and direct man with a no-nonsense attitude. If he wanted to converse with her privately, then the matter must be of substance. She gave Jon and Anna a perplexed and apprehensive look, which the married couple mirrored. The atmosphere tensed significantly.

Daniel sensed Doris's hesitancy and irresoluteness in leaving and grabbed her hand. "Just follow me, Doris. Please!" he pleaded softly. So she did.

Daniel led Doris through the crowd of people still mingling outside the church. A few people smiled at the pair as they walked past them. Daniel guided Doris down the church stairs. He steered her along the windy hillside toward a charming chalky-white gazebo. It was vacant as most people were still inside the church. The faint melody of the church choir could still be heard in the distance as Daniel and Doris walked alongside each other.

"Close your eyes," Daniel told Doris as they began nearing the alluring formation.

"Close my eyes? Are you kidding?"

"Don't you trust me, Doris?"

This question caught her off-guard. She and Daniel hadn't been on good terms for years now. However, during all this time, she never doubted his intentions for even a single passing second. She had always trusted Daniel and would continue to do so till she drew her last breath.

"Of course, I trust you," she said slowly.

"Good! Then close your eyes. I have a surprise for you!"

"Right then, as you wish!"

She closed her eyes, and Daniel held her hand more firmly, carefully leading her toward the gazebo. He guided her as they climbed the small steps near the bottom of the structure and didn't let go of her until she was standing in the middle of its circular floor made of polished wood.

"Can I open my eyes?" Doris asked once they had come to a halt.

"Just a few seconds," Daniel promised.

He then looked outside the entrance of the gazebo, where Mr. Simon was stationed at a distance. He pointed toward the rear end of the gazebo, and Daniel turned around to find the bouquet that Mr. Simon was carrying earlier placed upon a small granite bench. A tiny wireless speaker was also placed positioned beside it. He quickly picked up the fragrant bunch of flowers and returned to face Doris, who waited patiently in the center. He then gave the thumbs-up sign to Mr. Simon, who returned the gesture.

"Okay, you can open your eyes," Daniel told Doris.

As soon as Doris registered the fact that Daniel was standing in front of her with a huge bouquet of her favorite flowers in his hands, she was utterly and altogether astounded. She could not believe her eyes. Since the moment she set foot in Iceland, Daniel's behavior and attitude toward her had been extremely cold and frigid.

"What are you doing?" she asked him with a confused expression.

"Happy belated anniversary!" he smiled.

"Oh my God! It was last week. You remembered!" she exclaimed.

"Forty-six," he said as he looked at her ardently.

"Forty-six," she laughed. "That is right. Very good! What's gotten into you?"

"Let's just say a little birdie talked some long-due sense into me," Daniel let out a small chuckle before his face fell."

I'm so sorry, Doris. I have no excuse for my behavior. I've been…" Doris covered his lips with her fingers, stopping him.

"There's no need for apologies," she told him.

"Well, then, can I dance with you, like the first time we met at our fraternity dance?" Daniel asked.

"Fine, but where's the music?" she asked.

"It's right here," Daniel said as he pulled out his phone and clicked it toward the speaker. Their song from forty-five years ago started playing. The song was Keep On Loving You by the band REO Speedwagon.

Tears instantly pooled in Doris's eyes as she placed her hand in Daniel's. They danced and swayed in the bright sunlight, detached from the rest of the world. All their troubles and pain seemed to fade away in that moment as a dazzling haze overpowered their emotions. Every cherished and happy moment that they had experienced in all the years of their marriage flashed through their minds, and all their burdens seemed lighter.

CHAPTER 14
THE BIGGEST DEAL

A METALLIC GRAY SUV was parked outside the vast expanse of Jon's ranch. A tall chauffeur dressed in a sophisticated black suit carried two bags outside the open front doors. He placed them in the SUV's spacious trunk and leaned against the car, waiting for the passengers.

After just a few minutes had passed, Jon, Daniel, Dorris, and Anna emerged from inside the homestead. The two brothers descended the front steps of the porch and started making their way toward the vehicle stationed at a small distance. Doris and Anna, on the other hand, didn't follow them immediately. Instead, they decided to linger near the ranch's entrance for a little while longer as Doris hugged Anna goodbye.

"Are you going to be all right?" Anna asked her.

"To be completely honest with you, I'm not sure. Everything happened so fast. It was surprising," Doris admitted with a sigh.

However, she still looked positively radiant and contented. Getting back together with Daniel had been a source of huge joy and exhilaration.

"I know," Anna told her. "Please let us know how things go and if there's anything we can do."

"You and Jon's support really does help me so much!" Doris said.

They broke away from the hug and looked over at Jon and Daniel, who were engaged in a conversation of their own.

"Who would have guessed that these past weeks would turn out this way, huh?" Daniel mused.

"Not me!" Jon exclaimed. "Before you leave, however, I wanted to thank you for coming here and for our conversation and also for listening to me."

"I should be the one thanking you. You were right… about being fair to Doris."

Daniel's admission filled Jon's heart with joy.

"Come here, big brother!" he said as he hugged Daniel.

Daniel, who always found it difficult to express his emotions, had a hard time embracing Jon and pulled away quickly.

"One day, we'll have a real hug, brother to brother," Jon told him. Daniel was at a loss for words after hearing that. Therefore, Jon continued talking.

"We all care about you so much, Daniel. All these years when you haven't been here, we've still missed you immensely. Let's not let that happen again, okay?"

Doris came over from the ranch's entrance to join the two of them on their journey to the car. She walked alongside Daniel, and when they reached the SUV, she embraced Jon, bidding him goodbye.

"Jon, thanks for everything. You have been such a great help!"

"Wouldn't have it any other way," replied Jon.

After a few seconds, Dagur came running out of the house, followed by Magnus. The little boy sprinted toward Daniel and gave him a big hug.

"When are you coming back?" he asked Daniel. "We never went fishing."

"Hopefully soon. You're such a smart kid. Keep it up."

He then proceeded to hug Doris, who squeezed him tight.

A few moments and many well wishes later, Daniel and Doris were strapped in the backseat of the SUV. Jon, Anna, and Dagur waved to the departing couple and stood by the ranch's entrance until their car was well out of sight.

As the car swerved on to the road, both Doris and Daniel stared at the beautiful landscapes and vast green plains that they were leaving behind. Doris rolled down the window and allowed the fresh Icelandic air to caress her face one last time as they rolled into the exquisite break of day.

* * *

Daniel lounged upon one of the dining chairs as he skimmed through the day's news. With a newspaper in one hand and a hot cup of tea in the other, Daniel appeared more relaxed than he had been in an exceptionally long time. There were no creases lining his forehead and no frown adorning his mouth. Instead, a warm smile graced his expression, his face emanating a healthy glow. The bright Boston sunlight filtering through a nearby window fell upon one side of Daniel's profile, illuminating it further.

Doris was seated on the other side of the table. She looked equally radiant as she chewed on a toast whilst reading on her iPad. After a few blissful and exuberant moments, Daniel glanced at his watch and registered the time. He finished his tea and placed the newspaper on the table as he stood up to leave.

"Got to go to work, dear," he said as he walked to Doris's side of the table. He bent down and gave her a quick kiss on her cheek.

"You don't have to go to work," Doris interjected.

"The company doesn't run itself," Daniel told her.

"You got plenty of people doing a fine job, Daniel. I'm sure they can manage without you."

"I can't just leave so abruptly, honey. I'm easing out, slowly shifting the responsibility on the workers. It's going to work out better this way."

"It's not happening fast enough," Doris remarked with a sigh.

"But it is finally happening. I promise you!" Daniel smiled at her. He bent down and kissed her once more before making his way toward the apartment's door.

Daniel's office was on the topmost floor of the building. It was large and spacious with a huge glass window overlooking the bustling Boston roads and facing towering skyscrapers. Daniel was seated at his desk, with Mr. Simon and Phil Wood on the opposite side.

"How are we doing in Vegas?" Daniel asked.

"We just heard back from Rodney Casino. Something's off. I think they are playing us," Phil Wood informed.

"Damn it. I want that deal to go through," Daniel swore as a beat of silence passed between the three men. "We should go to New York and put some pressure on them. We can't let them continue this ploy."

"We can also leak the story," Phil Wood voiced, "that would put more pressure on them."

Daniel gave Phil Wood's idea a thought and then nodded. At that exact moment, his intercom buzzed as the voice of his assistant broke through the silence.

"Mr. Pallson, your eleven o'clock appointment is here," Laura announced.

"I don't remember making any appointments. Who is it?" Daniel asked.

"It's Reverend Adams. Miss Doris set it up," Laura informed him.

"Can it be canceled?" Daniel questioned hopefully.

"You already canceled on her last week, sir."

Daniel grimaced at these words and glanced toward the two men, who quickly stood up.

"I'll take care of it," Mr. Simon offered as he got out of his chair.

"No, it's alright! I can manage. Send her in, Laura," Daniel instructed grudgingly.

"Yes, sir!" Laura said before the intercom went quiet.

Reverend Adams entered the room as Mr. Simon and Phil Wood were exiting. Daniel stood up and shook the Reverend's hand.

"We meet again, hopefully under better circumstances!" she commented.

"Yes, indeed! My apologies for postponing last week. It's been busy catching up after I got back."

"Very understandable," Reverend Adams mentioned. "Doris told me you were considering retiring. Is that true?"

"I'm working on it." Daniel smiled as the two of them made their way toward Daniel's desk and took their places opposite one another.

Daniel's assistant, Laura, walked in at this moment. She was an attractive young woman in her early thirties with curly auburn hair and light brown eyes. She offered a glass of water to the reverend and proceeded to move toward Daniel's side of the table, where she stationed herself at his side.

"How have you been?" Reverend Adams asked once she set down the glass of cold water.

"Better, since Doris moved back to the house," he told her.

"Doris called me a few days ago. She told me that she is highly optimistic with regard to your relationship and that you recently made an important stride toward resolving your differences."

"She's right. We have indeed."

"That's excellent. Since you both are communicating with each other in a more effective manner now, I'm sure she told you that she wants you to see me. She believes now to be a good time."

"Yes, I am aware of that. She made it reasonably and entirely too clear that if I refused to see you, she would not move back."

"So, how do you expect this to go forward?" Reverend Adams asked.

"Reverend Adams, I am sure you are a very practical woman. Am I right?"

"I believe you are right. I am a practical woman."

"Great! So why don't you come by maybe once a month? I, in turn, will make sure your church gets some very meaningful and substantial anonymous donations. It'll be our little secret. Doris will be happy and contented, and it will also prove to be advantageous for you. What do you say?"

"Mr. Pallson, this is not how it works. If you don't want to make an honest effort, that is fine by me. However, you have to be true to Doris, because I will not lie to her, and neither will I allow you to make such requests. This is wrong and reprehensible."

"Ah! And I thought you said you were a practical woman."

"I am, but only when false pretenses are not involved. I will let myself out. And I was hopeful we could meet with a fresh start. Thank you for your time, Mr. Pallson." Reverend Adams sighed as she got out of her chair and made her way toward the office door. Daniel watched her as she left, his eyes fixed on the back of her head. Few people had ever talked to him like that, and her reaction made him very uncomfortable, knowing the possible fallout if the reverend contacted Doris about what had just occurred.

Laura, on the other hand, silently witnessed the whole exchange. She was dumbfounded and shocked at what she had heard. She quietly followed the reverend out of the office.

Back at home, Doris reclined on the blue-linen sofa placed in the middle of the living room as she surfed through all the different channels on her television. She had been at it for the past fifteen minutes and still had not found something enjoyable to watch. As she passed through CNBC, she quickly went back, as something on the channel had caught her eye. It was the newscaster, Jon Marshall. He was in his late fifties with neat gray hair, a strong jaw, and bright-green eyes. He was delivering news about a merger.

"We have just received a breaking news," he vocalized fluently. "It's just been reported that Daniel 'Big Deal' Pallson has yet again lived up to his nickname. Sources tell us his company is negotiating with a Las Vegas-based Rodney Casinos. We have been informed that Mr. Pallson aims to purchase the entire company for somewhere around 145 dollars a share, which would make this about a twenty-seven-billion-dollar acquisition, thus the biggest casino takeover in history. Both companies have yet to comment upon this buyout. Investors, however, have faith in Mr. Pallson, and the shares of the company are on the rise…"

Doris could not hear anymore. She turned off the television set as irritation and exasperation breached her control. She picked up her phone and immediately called Daniel. There was no answer. She called him again, but the outcome remained the same. She tossed her phone on the sofa and threw her hands in the air. She was extremely frustrated and disheartened. After she had a few minutes to calm her wits, she went to the study and turned on her computer. In the search bar, she typed in "Rodney Casino Merger" and read through all the latest news and articles pertaining to the issue. While she was engrossed in the scouring of information regarding her husband's deal, she heard her phone ring. She made her way to the living room and picked up her phone from the sofa, where she hurled it a few minutes ago. It displayed Daniel's name. She answered the call.

"Hello," she said.

"Hi, Doris, honey! Just missed your call," Daniel said from the other end.

"Don't 'Doris honey' me. Is this Rodney casino thing true?"

This question made Daniel hesitate.

"Now let me explain," he began, but Doris cut across him.

"Just answer my question, Daniel. Is it true? Yes or no?"

"It's not that simple." He tried to make her understand.

"Well, then come home and explain it. NOW!" she fumed.

"Honey, maybe in about an hour and a half. I have to go to a board meeting…" He heard a beat. "Doris, are you there?"

Doris had already hung up. This annoyed Daniel, who put his phone back inside his coat pocket. He held his head in his hands. However, he let go instantly as his assistant Laura entered the room.

"Mr. Pallson, the entire board is in the conference room. They're waiting for you," she informed him.

"OK, I'll be right in," he told her. "Also, Laura, would you mind going down to see the florist in the lobby and picking out a nice flower bouquet?"

"Of course," she said as she left the office, closing the door behind her.

* * *

Later that day, as Daniel returned home from the office, he was greeted by a disgruntled Doris. She was reading a book and did not look up when Daniel entered the room.

"Hello, my love!" Daniel called in an extra sugary voice. "How was your day today?"

Doris looked up at his question, and her eyes were instantly drawn toward the giant bouquet of flowers and expensive bottle of wine in his hands.

"Don't you dare try to bribe me with flowers and wine, Daniel," she warned him. "You completely broke your word. They are calling it the biggest deal ever. That does not sound like slowing down to me."

Daniel shook his head and was tremendously alarmed when he noticed the packed suitcases placed beside the door.

"Are you planning to go somewhere?" he questioned his wife cautiously.

"Yes, to Mars, as far as you are concerned."

"What do you mean by that? Are you leaving me again? You can't do this to me, Doris!" he pleaded, but Doris did not even bother to reply. She simply stared at him, searching his face.

"Trust me, please!" he continued. "This is the best deal I have ever done, and I promise it will be my last! It is a dream deal that will make my legacy."

"What is wrong with you? You just had a major heart attack, Daniel. Your work should not be more important to you than your life. And honestly, why do you even want me back? Why do you want me to stay?"

"Because I love you, Doris. I could not have done any of this without you."

"Then you should've listened to me. I warned you that I would be gone for good if you broke your word again." She tried to make Daniel remember his promise.

"You have to trust me, this one last time," he begged.

A deafening silence descended upon the room as they both stared at each other. Daniel wanted Doris to be supportive and understanding. He needed her to stand by his side with an encouraging smile as he conquered the business world. Doris, on the other hand, just wished for her husband's long life. She placed his health and well-being upon the highest pedestal. She did not consider his financial and material successes to be as important. Their priorities were directly at odds with each other. They both stared at one another with pleading eyes, hoping that the other one would budge. It was no use.

"How do you think it makes me feel," Doris muttered quietly after a few prolonged seconds, "when during an interview you say that dying behind your desk would bring you happiness?"

"When did I say that?" Daniel asked.

"A few years ago," she told him as she continued to speak. "Every time I think about that statement of yours, my heart shatters into a million tiny pieces. When I realize that my husband, who I have loved and cherished so dearly all my life, wants his last moments to come to pass behind a piece of wood rather than by my side, it rips my soul to shreds."

"I am a different man now, Doris," he declared.

"I highly doubt that," Doris replied as she marched out of the room. She came back after a few seconds with Daniel's pillow and his toothbrush in her hands. She placed them on a nearby counter, next to the flowers and the bottle of wine.

"Isabel just cleaned your favorite guest room. Good night!"

With this, Doris walked out of the living room and into her bedroom. She closed the door and locked it from inside.

Even though he had just been thrown out of his room, Daniel let out a sigh of relief. This was because he knew that the situation could have turned out to be a lot worse. He had no clue what he would have done if Doris would have decided to leave him again. He, therefore, picked up his pillow and toothbrush and made his way toward the guest room.

The next morning, Daniel awoke a little later than his usual time. He did not have his alarm clock in the guest room and had slept in. The curtains in the guest room were not drawn, and bright sun rays were falling upon the satin bedspread. As Daniel arose from his deep slumber, the first thought that came to his mind concerned Doris. After last night's argument, he wanted to make sure that he was still on good terms with his wife. He quickly got out of bed and slipped his feet into the soft woolen slippers that were placed on the ground just beside his bed. He yawned a great yawn and put on his robe, tightening it around his waist. He then left the room, proceeding toward the hallway.

As soon as he entered the living room, he noticed that Doris's luggage that was placed next to the door was gone. His mind instantly jumped to the worst possibility. Had Doris left him? Had she abandoned him in the middle of the night? He scurried in the direction of their bedroom with all possible haste.

"Doris," he called out. "Doris, where are you?"

He opened the bedroom door, and his heart sank. She wasn't in there.

"Doris! Doris!" he called out even louder this time.

He checked all the other rooms, panic-stricken and in a frenzy, but she was nowhere to be found. His biggest fear had come true. He reached for his phone and quickly called Doris's cell. It went straight to voicemail.

"This is Doris. I can't currently answer your call, but please leave your message."He had no idea what to do or where to look. He felt hopeless and dejected. Suddenly, the garden door opened, and the noise of someone entering the hallway reached Daniel's ears. He quickly ran in that direction, and to his utter and extreme relief, it was Doris.

She was wearing her walking outfit with a hot tea from a vendor across the street.

She was wearing a hat and her gardening gloves, which she was in the process of taking off.

"Doris, where have you been?" Daniel asked.

"On one of the longest thinking walks ever."

"I didn't see your luggage."

"I unpacked everything in the morning since you decided to sleep in today, apparently," she teased as she strolled into the kitchen. Daniel followed her.

She unzipped her sweat top and turned on the faucet, cleaning her hands.

"I also had some time to think about us," Doris told Daniel.

"And what it is that you've thought?"

"I've realized I am not going to teach an old dog anything. You are too set in your ways. You are not a child. I cannot scold you or force you to do anything that you don't want to," she continued. "But you need to understand that I won't stand dishonesty either. If you promise me something, I will hold you accountable if you break it. But if you want to die at your desk by working too much, I won't be able to stop you."

"I don't want to kill myself, Doris."

"All I ask is that you honor your commitments, the ones you made in Iceland."

"You mean seeing Reverend Adams?"

"Yes. Have you even met her once since we came back?"

"Yes, I did."

"Well, how did it go?"

"It went fine. I am seeing her again next week."

"Good, thank you, Daniel! How often are you two meeting?"

Daniel thought for a moment before answering this question.

"We're working that out," he finally told her.

Doris beamed at her husband as she pulled him into a hug. She gave him a quick kiss on his cheek.

"Thank you! I still have some work left in the garden. I'll be outside," she told him as she made her way toward the door.

The second Doris left the apartment, Daniel pulled out his phone and frantically called his assistant. She picked it on the third ring, but it felt more like it took twice that.

"Laura, please get me Reverend Adams now."

CHAPTER 15
REALITY OF SUFFERING

The cool Boston air caressed Daniel's face as he stepped out of the backseat of his pristine SUV. The morning was bright and clear as the sun hung high in the extraordinary blue sky. Today was his meeting with Reverend Adams, and saying that Daniel was unenthusiastic about it would be an understatement. However, despite his obvious disregard and disinterest, he had pulled up to the church in a timely fashion. The sole motivator that had encouraged him to attend this meeting was Doris, along with the fear of her leaving.

As Daniel gazed upward to get a look at the church building, he was amazed by the grandeur of the architecture. It was shaped like a cathedral with tall steeples and tapering conical spires. The exterior walls of the church were painted white and gold, with stained glass windows and enormous wooden doors. It was evidently the most beautiful building Daniel had ever laid his eyes upon. After he had gotten used to the church's immaculate beauty and its glorious aura, he proceeded to climb the long line of stairs leading to the front door. Even the railings beside the white marble steps were embellished with striking golden carvings.

As he was admiring the artistry of the church's architecture, a man dressed in a crisp suit walked by along with a young woman who appeared to be his girlfriend. They recognized Daniel and walked up to him.

"Hello," the girl greeted as she stopped to face Daniel. "Mr. Pallson, me and my boyfriend are both enrolled in the MBA program at BC, and we're big fans of yours. Please, can we get a picture with you? It would mean a lot."

Daniel was not happy with this request and felt annoyed, if not inconvenienced. He simply wanted to meet the reverend and get back to work as quickly as humanly possible. However, he did not express his irritation.

"Big fans, huh? That's nice to hear. Let's do it!" He smiled at them.

"Thanks so much, Mr. Pallson," the boyfriend chimed in as the girl pulled her phone out of her bag and swiftly clicked a selfie with the three of them in the frame.

"No worries! I wish you both successful lives and thriving careers," Daniel said. "Remember to make BC proud. I'm not sure you know, but I also got my MBA from there."

"Yes, of course we know, Mr. Pallson," the girl said this time.

After exchanging a few more words, the couple departed, and Daniel continued climbing the stairs. He entered the church through the massive front doors and was once again spellbound by the church's splendor. It was large and spacious. The high ceilings of the building were covered in paintings and murals, while tall pillars and posts ascended vertically from all sides. A huge sculpture of Jesus was situated near the front of the room. Daniel walked across the aisle, with long rows of polished pews on both sides. He was looking to ask for directions to the reverend's office when he spotted her standing outside a wooden door near the back of the church. She was waiting for him. He waved his hand at her as he walked in her direction.

"I see you're on time, Mr. Pallson," she commented as Daniel came closer. He shook hands with the reverend. His demeanor was humbler this time around, and he exhibited a lot more respect.

"Of course, wouldn't want to keep you waiting, Reverend." He smiled at her. Reverend Adams led Daniel into her office and seated herself in a wooden chair behind her desk. She motioned for Daniel to make himself comfortable in the seat opposite hers.

"Please have a seat, Mr. Pallson," she told him.

Once Daniel took his spot, an uncomfortable silence fell around the room. He didn't know how to begin the conversation, and it seemed as though the reverend wanted him to speak first. He, therefore, decided to occupy his time by looking around the office. It was a small but cozy circular office. It had a wooden floor and cream-colored walls. Upon those walls hung different frames, each showcasing the reverend's numerous achievements. Daniel glanced at the walls filled with diplomas from various universities.

"Daniel, please. I can see why Doris thinks highly of you, why she believes that you are the right person to talk to, having earned all these sheepskins," Daniel uttered finally.

"Sheepskins?" Reverend Adams repeated with a soft chuckle. "I haven't heard that in a while."

Daniel's eyes fell upon a nearby frame, within which a diploma for a master's degree in psychology was enclosed.

The frame beside it held a degree for a Ph.D. in philosophy. Daniel was incredibly impressed.

"Master's in psychology and grief counseling from NYU, a Ph.D. in philosophy from B.C. On top of that, you're a woman of the cloth. Very impressive! It seems you truly are the person for the job," Daniel commended her.

"Why is that, Mr. Pallson?" Reverend Adams inquired.

Daniel thought about the question for a minute before answering. "Well, it's mainly because most of my issues relating to Doris are…spiritual. It's safe to say that I am not a religious person, and with your background I feel like you are going to be the closest thing to a famous philosopher or a representative of God that I can talk to," he finished.

This time, Reverend Adams laughed.

"So, I'm representing Socrates, Kierkegaard, and the Holy Trinity?"

They both cackled at her amusing response.

"How about Freud too?" Daniel further added.

"Funny you mention Freud. I'm not sure if you know, but he was among the very first to study human grief."

"Well, I don't think there's anything that guy didn't dip his feet in. Sex too, right?"

Reverend Adams did not appreciate this comment, especially within the confines of a church. She gave him a scornful look before saying, "Freud was an astounding philosopher. It's tragic some people don't realize that. I hope I do him proud."

"We will see, Reverend Adams. We will see."

"Indeed, we will," she said as she got out of her chair and reached for a coffee pot perched upon a tiny table nearby.

"Would you like a cup of coffee?" she asked Daniel as she poured herself one.

"No, thanks," Daniel declined. "Just had some on the way over."

The reverend nodded and reclined back in her seat once again.

"So, what do you want to talk about?" she questioned.

"I don't know. You tell me. What did Doris say?"

"She mainly stressed the fact that you struggle with perennial depression and obsessive guilt. She also told me you lack all sense of spirituality."

"As you are well aware, I'm here for her. So, if she believes that these should be the issues we cater to in our sessions, then that's what we should do," Daniel expressed his thoughts.

"I believe that you should be the one to present for yourself. That's the idea, anyway. I simply want what's best for you."

"Alright then! What Doris said makes sense to me. Spirituality, depression, whatever."

Reverend Adams believed this to be acceptable. "Good, then I suggest we meet two times a week for the next ten weeks. I need to know you are committed."

This suggestion made Daniel's eyes fly wide open. "You're kidding, right?" he said. "Ten weeks? Twice a week? That's impossible."

"Nothing's impossible, Daniel, if you truly commit to it."

"Well, Reverend, I am committing to this. Why do you think I'm seated in front of you? It's just that I have a business to run and a company to manage. I have to travel very frequently. I can't stay rooted in Boston for the next ten weeks," he tried to explain.

Reverend Adams was a reasonable woman. "That should not be a problem. I'm sure you have Skype or some equivalent. We can have virtual sessions when you are not in town," she offered.

Daniel thought about this for a minute. "Yeah, that's a good idea," he finally decided.

"Great! We will work on the scheduling soon," Reverend Adams announced, and Daniel nodded.

"Good luck on all of this," Daniel interjected suddenly.

"What do you mean by that?" she asked with a confused expression.

"Well, it's you and Doris's big wish to lead me into a utopian world of contentment and relaxation, so good luck with that," he explained.

"Daniel, if any good comes from our meetings, it will be solely dependent upon your effort. But at the same time I need you to understand that there are no expectations. This is wholly and completely your choice."

Daniel pondered her words for a full minute as silence descended upon the room.

"Do you know what I believe in? Something the existence of which no one can deny," he questioned at last.

"What is it?" the reverend replied.

Daniel promptly got out of the chair and walked around the table toward a blank chalkboard. He grabbed a long piece of chalk and began scribbling something. Reverend Adams spun around in her seat to glance at him. Upon the board, Daniel inscribed the letter D in a capital letter, followed by I, then C, then H, followed by O, then T, O, M, I…

"Dichotomies," the Reverend read.

"Very good, Reverend, yes, dichotomies."

"Something that contains contradictory elements," she mused as Daniel put down the chalk but remained standing.

"Exactly, Reverend," Daniel agreed. "But I'm not talking about the benign ones like sun and rain, which make a pretty little rainbow. I'm talking about the countless tragic ones on this planet related to so much inhumane pain and suffering every day.

"For example?"

"Examples? Okay, a few of the countless. Just to start, why is it so common for love to somehow become hate. Or a happy child ends up in a cancer ward enduring chemotherapy, fighting for their life. And parents suffers the loss of a child, no matter the cause or how old they are. The biggest dichotomy of it all: the supposed 'good God' you represent and all that suffering."

Reverend Adams was completely taken aback by Daniel's words and paused before she replied.

"Cat got your tongue, Reverend?" Daniel asked.

"The question you raised does not have a simple answer. It can be difficult to explain," she said.

"Try me, Reverend," he challenged.

Suddenly, the assistant, Jamie, comes across the intercom system.

"Sorry to interrupt, Reverend," says Jamie.

Daniel could not hide his frustration with the interruption.

"Sorry to interrupt, Reverend," the girl said in a small voice.

"Yes, Jamie. What is it?"

"I wanted to remind you about your group session at 11 a.m. It's just that the group is here, and they're waiting for you downstairs in the primary meeting room," Jamie informed.

"Oh, yes, thank you! I'll be right down," she told Jamie before she diverted her attention toward Daniel.

"Mr. Pallson, I'm so sorry, but we're gonna have to stop here today," she informed him.

Daniel, who was already frustrated at the interruption, couldn't hide his exasperation. "Really?" he asked. "You're gonna leave me hanging on the best part of our conversation today?"

"I'm afraid so, although I promise we will resume from here in the next meeting," she assured him as she got out of her chair and grabbed a folder that had been sitting in front of her on the table. She pushed it into Daniel's hands.

"What is this?" he asked.

"This is very important to make our arrangement work. It's a very standardized questionnaire that you need to fill in before our next meeting, no later than that."

"Seriously, Reverend," Daniel scoffed. "Are you my guidance counselor in middle school?"

"Please, I will explain everything in due time. For now, make sure that you complete the questionnaire."

Reverend Adams then led Daniel out of her office.

"Good start today," she commented while they walked side by side toward the church's nave.

"Start to what?" remarked Daniel sarcastically.

* * *

It was late afternoon in Iceland when a phone rang inside the Pallson ranch. Jon heard the ring while he was painting the outside fence, with Dagur helping him. He cleaned his hands with a paint-stained cloth as he proceeded toward the front door. He entered the house and answered the phone.

"Hello," he said into the speaker. "Hello?"

"Hey! Jon, it's Daniel. Do you have time to talk?"

Jon could not help but be surprised at hearing his brother's voice.

"Oh yeah, sure! Of course, I have time. I was just working outside with Dagur, but I can talk."

"Good. So is everything alright?"

"Yeah, everything's well and good. Hey, listen, I saw this news on the television about a big merger…" Jon asked as he walked back out.

"Uh, yes."

"How did Doris react to it?"

"I think she is okay with it." He knew she wasn't.

"Hope you are right about that. Just please don't blow this with her, especially now," Jon said as he carefully worked on the fence.

"I'm not. I'm even seeing Dr. Adams now."

"Really?"

"Yes, no guarantee, but I'm doing it," Daniel shrugged his shoulders as he informed Jon.

Jon kept working on the fence while Dagur held the fence in place, "Daniel, please give this one the effort it deserves."

"I will, Jon, don't worry," Daniel reassured him.

As they continued their conversation, Anna stepped on the patio and called out to Jon and Dagur for dinner. "Jon! Dagur! Dinner is ready. You can continue gardening afterward."

"I hear Anna calling you. I gotta go too. Will be in touch."

"Okay. It was good to hear your voice, Daniel. Take care."

"Enjoy your dinner, Jon, and give my regards to Anna and Dagur."

"Will do."

And with that, Jon hung up the phone and placed the phone back in his pocket. Before making his way into the house with Dagur, he took a moment to admire the garden's beauty. As he quickly made his way to the patio, where Anna had set up a beautifully arranged table, Jon expressed his gratitude toward his wife. "Thank you for the amazing dinner, dear."

"You're most welcome." Anna smiled as Jon gave her a kiss on her cheek. "Who were you talking to?"

"Daniel called. He is having some issues again, but I think he will work it out. In fact, he is even seeing Reverend Adams now," Jon continued. "Oh, and he gave his regards to both of you."

"Really? He actually met with the reverend?" Anna was slightly shocked.

"That was precisely my reaction," Jon smiled as he took a bite from his plate.

"Well, at least it's good to see him trying." Anna smiled warmly. "Now, let's eat dinner before it gets cold."

As the evening drew to a close, Jon felt for his brother, hoping that everything would turn out great for him now that he was trying.

* * *

It was just another morning, another day at the office, but something was different. Today, Daniel was having his next meeting with Reverend Adams since their last discussion. Sitting face to face with Daniel, Reverend Adams started the discussion.

"So, Daniel, we will start right from where we finished the other day."

"Yes, Reverend. I was waiting for your answer."

"Daniel, suffering, or the dichotomy you refer to with respect to a 'good God,' is in many ways probably the most asked question by many."

"Big surprise." Daniel smirked.

"The reality of suffering, however, does not disprove the existence of an omnipotent God."

"Why?"

"Are you familiar with the term 'free will?'" Reverend Adams asked, raising her eyebrows.

"With respect to God?" Daniel asked, confusion evident in his eyes.

"Yes. If a person has free will, he or she is able to make their own decisions without being controlled by fate. This also applies to all sins."

"Reverend, I don't understand where you are going here."

"Daniel, God created human suffering but is not responsible for it."

"Even if your free will theory is assumed correct, that does not explain all those innocent people suffering the pain they never deserved nor could've kept at bay since they had no free will, to begin with, so your answer is not complete."

"I think I can complete my answer, but that would be over more time as we dig into some things that will help me explain."

"Of course, Reverend, as long as it doesn't too closely resemble the often-common easy answer by a clergy that we just don't understand the pain and suffering here on this earth but will surely understand in the life after this one, then it's okay."

"Okay, first, our work must deal primarily with the raw emotion of grief and suffering you have experienced for so long."

"Okay, whatever that implies." Daniel shrugged.

"Well, let me just…" The reverend lifted her bag, searched for something inside it, and took out a file. And then she opened up the file with the questionnaire Daniel had completed.

"Oh, the questionnaire was completely answered. Hope you are proud of me, Reverend."

"Mr. Pallson, please, this is no time for sarcasm. The results were consistent with what I expected."

"Alright, go ahead, Reverend."

"Mr. Pallson, you have what is called Persistent Complex Bereavement Disorder."

"And what's that?" Daniel leaned back in his chair and furrowed his eyebrows.

"Well, in layman's terms, you have among the longest and most severe grief cases I have ever been aware of."

"Is that really a surprise?" he asked as he grinned.

"You know how I explained to you the commonly used Kubler Ross 5 stages of grief? Since Thomas passed, you have not gotten past stage 3 of the detachment and depression stage. You have been stuck at this level for decades when most people in your situation would be able to get to the acceptance and meaning in life at least by three to five years," Reverend Adams explained.

"I can't believe anyone with my circumstance could just go about normally in even three to five years," Daniel replied.

"Doris took about four years before I saw a definite ability to deal with the associated anxiety inside her. It's amazing you are able to function in the way you have this many years, the way you have managed between your marriage and your well-flourishing business…"

Daniel interrupted before the reverend could complete her sentence, "Never thought about the time. Just been living day to day with the angst, whether it has a name or clinical explanation or whatever."

"Never thought of seeking help?" Reverend Adams inquired, pinpointing as she tilted her head, raising an eyebrow.

"Help? There was nothing anybody could have done except bring my son back."

"Some sort of help?" she said again, emphasizing the word "help."

"Doris tried it, and obviously that didn't work, so nobody could HELP." Daniel continued, "I grew up as a grandson and a great-grandson of Viking fishermen, and my father was a bare-knuckled farmer and mechanic who just sucked everything up. The only way I ever knew too."

"Daniel, it's never too late," Reverend Adams said, sorrow in her voice.

"Reverend, I am sixty-nine years old with significant cardiovascular disease, including a recent major heart attack. Not too late for what? I just don't want Doris to walk out that door with what little time I probably have left," Daniel said gloomily as he gazed at the reverend, desperate for an answer.

CHAPTER 16
ONE LAST TIME

The Rodney Casino conference room was spacious and sophisticated, situated on the 17th floor of the building, overlooking the city beneath. In the middle of the space was a long rectangular table with a series of chairs on each side. The walls were furnished with avant-garde paintings and abstract drawings, which stood out against the plain white backdrop. In one corner of the room was a bar stacked with numerous kinds and brands of alcoholic beverages.

Daniel was the first to enter the room, followed by Mr. Simon and Phil Wood. They took their seats on one side of the spread-out table. Shortly after, the owner of the casino, Rodney, entered the room. He was the exact same age as Daniel, though he looked much older. He had drooping eyes, sagging skin, dirty gray hair, and a shimmering gold tooth. He was accompanied by two younger associates. Before the three of them seated themselves on the opposite side, Rodney walked up to Daniel and shook hands with him enthusiastically. It was clear that the two of them had known each other for a long time.

Rodney initiated the conversation. "Daniel, how are you, my friend?" he began.

"Good, but I'll be better when we finish signing the deal," Daniel answered.

"No foreplay, huh? Just diving directly into the deep end," Rodney snickered as he walked toward the bar and poured himself a whiskey."

Want one?"Daniel shook his head, declining his offer. Rodney then made his way toward the table and settled down.

"Is everything alright, my friend? When was the last time you turned down a fine single malt blend?" Rodney commented.

"You don't want to know," Daniel remarked. "So, tell me, what's bothering you?"

"Loads of things!" Rodney sighed before continuing. "My wife is driving me crazy these days. She wants to have kids now."

"How old is your wife?" Daniel questioned.

"Thirty-one, the clock's ticking!"

"So, when the kid graduates high school, you'd be about ninety-five." Both men chuckled.

"We ain't no spring chickens anymore," Rodney said this time.

"So what are you going to do?" Daniel asked seriously, but Rodney changed the topic.

"Never mind that," he uttered. "Tell me about your health."

"Strong as an ox!" Daniel told him.

"I heard a different version."

"Don't believe everything you hear."

Rodney grinned before he asked, "How long are you planning to stay in charge day-to-day?"

This question made Daniel chortle. "Until I drop dead! Unless my wife has her say," he responded.

"So, let's say I sell to you, making this the biggest merger ever, and in one month you're back in the hospital. What will happen then?"

Daniel sensed that they were finally talking business. "I nearly died a few months ago, and it didn't affect my company one bit," he assured.

"Nearly being the operative word."

"No guts, no glory," Daniel said finally as he got out of his chair. Mr. Simon and Phil Wood mirrored him. He extended his hand toward Rodney, who shook it before Daniel and his accompanying partners left the room.

* * *

Daniel was furious. He was in the backseat of his SUV, with his driver in the front, trying to navigate through the crowded streets of New York City. He was shouting over his phone at Mr. Simon and Phil Wood, who were unfortunate enough to be at the receiving end of his anger.

"Call all the key shareholders," he commanded. "I want this matter dealt with by the end of the week. There is no way he is getting away with this."

As the two men responded to this injunction, Daniel could not continue listening. He ended the call and put down his cell phone. Instead, he clutched his chest. He was experiencing sharp pain in his chest, traveling down his arms to the tips of his fingers. He immediately reached for the medicine that Doris had carefully placed in the back pocket of his briefcase. He ingested the prescription drug and slowly felt the pain fading away. However, instead of going to the hospital for a checkup, Daniel decided to shake it off.

* * *

It was evening in Las Vegas. The sun hung low in the sky, and the city's tall skyscrapers reflected its vivid and fiery gleam. Daniel was exhausted as he entered his hotel room. He loosened his tie from his neck and pulled it off, throwing it upon the unsullied and spotless bedspread. Then he unfastened the top button of his shirt. His extreme tiredness and weariness were evident on his face. He had been in and out of meetings all day and did not get a chance to rest or relax for even a minute. Even now, instead of crashing upon his made bed and calling it a day, he was engaged in a conversation with Reverend Adams over Skype.

"Many of the brightest people in the world have believed that regardless of the religion a person chooses to follow he or she is always praying to the same God. The difference lies only in the interpretations," he finished expressing his thoughts.

"Yes and no. Let me give you some examples," the reverend said from the other end. "Hinduism, for instance, believes in an impersonal God. Buddhism, on the other hand, says that God exists within time. While Christianity exerts that God is not bound by time at all. Christians believe that God existed before time and, consequently, the universe."

She saw Daniel yawn on her laptop screen.

"Have you had any recurring dreams lately?" she asked.

"Not since we started," Daniel told her.

"Can you do me a favor?" she requested him.

"Name it," was Daniel's response.

"Each time you wake up, can you write down anything you remember from your dreams? No matter how insignificant it seems."

"I'll make notes on my phone like I do for many things."

"Whatever works best for you," she spoke. "You might be surprised how quickly we forget our dreams. I have some clinical experience in dream interpretation, so it might be possible for us to tap into something of use."

"Whatever floats our boat, Reverend," Daniel remarked before ending the call.

* * *

Doris was perched on the sofa beside Daniel, who was fast asleep. They were both watching Doris's favorite show about home makeovers and renovations when Daniel fell asleep. He had experienced a long day at work and felt overly drained and worn out by the time he reached his house. After he settled on the couch, it only took him a few minutes to drift into a deep slumber. Once again, the dream interrupted his peace.

Daniel was his current age, and he was fishing with a ten-year-old Thomas, who was sporting a fishing hat. He always donned this exact hat in each of Daniel's dreams. Magnus was standing alongside Thomas. As they stood by the flowing water, submerged to their knees, Daniel turned his attention toward his son.

"Tommy, I think I got him!" he called out.

"Dad, be careful. Don't lose it," Thomas told him as he came over to help Daniel out.

Magnus smiled at the pair as he asked, "Is it the big one?"

It was indeed the big one. Daniel had to grapple with the fish with all his strength as Thomas tried to be of assistance. Suddenly, Daniel handed the fishing rod to Thomas, and now the ten-year-old was the one fighting for control.

"I have been fighting this fish for years. This time, we got him," Daniel uttered.

"We've got to let her out a bit, and now we bring her back in. Here it comes," Thomas said happily.

"Yes, Son, there you go. You got it."

"Yes, and it is huge!" Magnus interjected.

Thomas continued to reel in the wriggling fish, but the line snapped due to the struggle, and the fish swam away, out of reach.

"Oh, damn! Not again," Daniel grunted.

All three of them looked extremely disappointed. Thomas was the most dejected. Tears welled up in his eyes as he looked up at Daniel.

"I'm so sorry, Dad. I screwed up," he whispered.

"No, you did not screw it up, Son. I have told you about this fish. It keeps getting away no matter how hard I try. It's not your fault!" Daniel tried to explain, but Thomas was persistent and woeful.

"No, Dad! I did, as I always do," he repeated.

"Stop that nonsense," Daniel exclaimed. "That is not true. It never was. Why can't you stop doing that to yourself, Son?"

"When are you going to quit blaming yourself…and Mom? I was old enough to know better. These kinds of things just happen. It was my fault. I got caught up with the wrong crowd. I didn't know better. But it is life. I just want you to know that I tried. I really did."

"I know you tried, Son. I know you did!" Daniel managed to say.

"I love you, and I want you to tell Mom that I will always love her. I have faith in you, Dad, just like you always had in me. Whatever happens, please never lose faith in a future where we are somehow together again. I have to go, Dad! I don't have a choice."

CHAPTER 17
SCREAMING AND SHOUTING

These were the last words Daniel heard Thomas speak before he woke up with a start. The dream shook him to the core, and he had to spend a few moments trying to figure out his surroundings. Even though he had experienced the same recurring dream countless times, it always had the same nerve-racking and disquieting effect.

"Did you have a nightmare, dear?" Doris asked from beside him.

"No, it's nothing," Daniel lied.

* * *

Daniel was once again seated in front of Reverend Adams in her office.

"Over the years, grief survivors such as yourself have asked me to interpret dreams like these," the reverend began. "We studied dreams in my psychology classes back in the day. The interpretation can be complex, and sometimes it can be risky to draw conclusions."

"So you feel more comfortable interpreting a book from two thousand years ago that many would consider contains impossible events?" Daniel asked.

"That's different."

"How is that different? Nobody can say you aren't a woman of conviction."

"What I mean, Daniel, is that I've never heard of someone who had the same recurrent dream for such an extended period of time. I will, therefore, say that seeking a meaningful answer from that dream can often be wishful thinking. So, I ask you, what would you like it to mean? Do you think that it is a message from your son? Or do you believe that it could be your own subconsciousness trying to rationalize the trauma and the suffering that you have experienced?"

"I don't know, Reverend. You tell me!"

"I always say that God can work—"

"In mysterious ways. That seems to be the standard answer when all else fails. My brother uses these exact same words quite often," he commented.

"Well, sounds like he believes these words and this ideology, exactly like I do," she told him softly. A moment of silence passed before the teverend spoke again."

What do Thomas's dreams have in common?"Daniel shrugged in response.

"He keeps telling you not to feel so guilty?" she continued, but Daniel still didn't say anything. "Doris told me that after Thomas was born, you said some kind of a God must exist because the beauty of a newborn can't be explained otherwise," she added further.

This drew a response from Daniel. "Yes, I recall I did," he told her.

"That's good. I also remember you saying that you became more accepting of religion until you lost Thomas."

"That was a long time ago," Daniel commented.

"I understand that. I'm just trying to put things into perspective," she said in return, and Daniel nodded.

"If you could talk to Thomas now," she questioned, "what do you think you would tell him?"

"It's not that simple," Daniel muttered quietly after a prolonged pause.

"Do you think you could've done anything differently?" she inquired.

"Of course."

"What do you think you could've done differently?"

"I could have saved his life!" Daniel fumed, anger seeping deep within his bones.

"And how would you have done that?" she tried to get him to answer.

However, Daniel, who was having a hard time keeping his emotions in check, simply said, "I don't have time for this."

"No, please, this is important. If you could go back in time, how would you save him?" she insisted, trying to reel out a response.

Daniel's phone vibrated. Daniel, who desperately wanted a way out of this conversation, picked it up.

"Hello!" he muttered into the speaker. "Damn it! I'll be there." He hung up."

Sorry, I have to leave," he told the reverend as he got out of the chair and started walking toward the door.

However, the reverend was not ready to give up.

"What would you have done?" she called out once more as Daniel exited the room. She sighed when the door slammed shut behind him. However, the very next second, the door burst open again, and Daniel entered.

"I would have been there for him," he responded loudly. "More than I was. I would have spied on his phone calls. I would have interrupted the conversations he had and the plans he made with the people who were bad for him. I would have done all of this and a thousand other taboo things because, as terrible as this sounds, it could have very well saved his life. I was his father, and I failed. I failed miserably and pathetically. Does that answer your question?"

He turned around, breathing heavily, and walked out the door. This time, the reverend followed him.

"Don't forget our final meeting tomorrow," she called out after him.

"I think our business is done here," he replied heatedly.

"Listen here, Mr. Big Deal Dan. Do not give up on our work now! I think you are so close to breaking through here. If you do break through, you will realize that you will still be able to make up for things with your family and all the things you have shut out for so long, and it will be something so great you can't even imagine! That will be the biggest deal of your life."

"Give me a break, Reverend!" Daniel said as he continued to walk forward without even turning around to face the reverend while talking.

* * *

Doris was in the kitchen, fixing dinner, while Daniel paced back and forth in the living room. He was talking on the phone with someone, and the conversation was getting increasingly vehement with every passing second. Doris could hear every word.

"I thought we had the main shareholders on our side? What the hell changed?" he questioned, his voice laced with anger.

He listened for a moment before resuming speech. "Of course, it has Rodney's fingerprints all over it. We have to find out who is still on our side."

He went silent again as he allowed the person on the other end to voice their concern.

"Find out who is behind this, and I mean right now! Good night," he uttered a few seconds later with finality ringing in his words.

When Doris walked into the room, she could see that Daniel was visibly upset. He was sitting on the couch with his head in his hands. She walked up to him.

"You can't keep this up. Your body won't be able to take much more. Your blood pressure is going to go through the roof." She once again attempted to make Daniel understand the graveness and the gravity of his condition.

"I'm okay," Daniel retorted.

"Come on, Daniel! It's time to let Phil Wood take over. He is totally and entirely capable, and you know it," she said.

"I agree with you, my love! But I need to see this deal through one last time. I'll pass the responsibility over to him once I'm assured that this project is finalized."

"Can I trust you?" she asked.

Daniel nodded, and even though he was more tired than he had ever been before, he managed to muster a small smile for his wife.

"For some reason," she told him, "I believe you this time. We're getting old and should enjoy the rest together."

Daniel nodded again and leaned in to kiss Doris, who happily kissed him back.

CHAPTER 18
THE BEST BET

DANIEL WAS SITTING on a park bench across the street from the Boston Commons area location of Reverend Adams's church. He had his arms stretched on both sides. He was basking in the sunlight, focused on all the live-action moments of the here and now. He watched as people hurried past him. He assumed that they were running off to work or just simply running. He gazed upon the mothers and their newborns sitting in the grass. And then he took his time observing the birds in the trees and the ducks sprinting nearby. It was just another normal day in most people's lives. Daniel looked blankly at a middle-aged man who was walking his dog. The dog wagged his tail at Daniel, who bent down to pet him. Afterward, he once again lifted his head toward the sky, feeling the warmth of the sun.

He could not remember the last time he felt this relieved. It was a feeling he had forgotten. He felt peaceful and relaxed. His gaze fell upon a man lounging on a similar bench at a distance. His granddaughter was perched upon his lap. Daniel could not help but admire the child's giggles and her liveliness. The man caught Daniel's eye and smiled at him.

"Sometimes it really is the little things in life, isn't it?" he called out. "I was lucky enough to learn that a long time ago."

"I wish we could all be so lucky," Daniel said with a friendly smile, meaning every word of it.

* * *

It was early in the morning when Daniel strolled past the open door to the reverend's office, where she was pouring herself a morning coffee.

"Wasn't so sure you would show up," she said once she saw Daniel walk in.

"Me neither," Daniel replied. "But there is something I must tell you. Today, for the first time in years, I woke up without the angst of so many years. I felt liberated and free. It was truly an amazing feeling."

"That's great, Daniel! Why do you think you felt this way?" asked Reverend Adams.

"I had the same dream again, and I woke up in cold sweat like I do every time. Everything in the dream was the same. Thomas uttered the same words about believing and having faith. But somehow this time I felt different. I have realized that in the future, regardless of the amount of time I have left, if I do indeed believe any hope for any future good is to conjure up faith, everything is possible. There is little to lose and maybe everything to gain. Maybe that's what Thomas was trying to say in the dreams. I need to have faith in myself, God, and the fact that so much, including connecting with Thomas, might be a possibility." Daniel had a strange glimmer in his eyes as he voiced these thoughts.

"Also, what contributed to me feeling this way was to think long and hard about you asking me not to be blinded like so many of my peers who have significant fortunes and power and who have developed a false know-it-all arrogance toward so much, especially religion, forgetting where they stand in reality, in the big picture. They forget that they are still a drop of water in the ocean. I think I became guilty of that arrogance long ago."

Reverend Adams beamed at him. "I am so happy for you, Daniel," she told him. "I've never seen you glow like this before."

"I don't ever remember feeling this way, Reverend. For some reason, it just feels right. It is all because of you and Doris."

"Well, in my line of work, you know I can't take any credit, which is fine, but thank you anyway." She smiled once more. "Daniel, I would like to give you something on our last meeting."

She looked in the topmost drawer of her desk and drew out a book. She handed it to Daniel. It was titled "Carrying On, A Guide to Survival Grief."

"Please read this when you get a chance," she continued.

"Is this your new book, Reverend?" Daniel asked, and she nodded in reply. "Thanks, I'll definitely read through it. Will you sign it for me?"

"Of course!" she said as she signed the book. After a few moments, Daniel turned to leave, but Reverend Adams stopped him.

"Hey, Daniel," she called out.

"What's that, Reverend?"

"If there is anything you need from me, don't hesitate to call, okay?"

"Thanks, Reverend! I wouldn't bet on it though."

"You know I'm not supposed to bet."

"Then you would be surprised to see some people who frequent my casinos," Daniel commented with a chuckle.

"I'm sure!" the reverend laughed.

They exchanged goodbyes as Daniel finally left the reverend's office with a huge smile on his face.

* * *

It had been a week since his conversation with the reverend, and Daniel was on a call in his office. He hung up the phone with a gloomy and sorrowful expression and buried his face in his hands. The only voice in the room was the opera playing on a nearby stereo.

A few seconds later, Mr. Simon came bursting through the doors and turned on the television.

"You better see this," he told Daniel.

On the television screen was a male newscaster named Pat Langley.

"Breaking news this morning. Let's go over to Susan on Wall Street," Pat told the audience as the camera cut to Susan Hernandez.

"Thank you, Pat. It is indeed very big news as the Justice Department has made a surprise move to place a complete halt on the Pallson Diversified-Rodney Casino merger. This merger was placed at a value of a whopping forty-eight billion dollars! However, Attorney General Bowman has clearly stated that such a deal would only lead to the creation of unfair monopolies."

Once again, the face of Pat Langley flashed across the screen. "This is as big as it gets, ladies and gentlemen," he announced. "Especially when Daniel Pallson is known to be a long-time friend of the president and is well-acquainted with numerous members of the Senate."

Daniel was shocked and dismayed by this news. He turned to Mr. Simon.

"Call an emergency board meeting as soon as possible. Latest by tomorrow. Video conference those who cannot be here," he instructed.

Mr. Simon nodded before he left, and Daniel diverted his attention toward the television screen. Susan Hernandez was speaking this time.

"That's right, Pat. Now, Pallson and Rodney Casinos can choose to fight the government on this, and it will be very interesting to see if they do. However, there have been various rumors regarding the fact that Rodney Casino has been attempting to pull out of the deal for a long time now. At any rate, if the deal does not go through, Daniel Pallson would be liable for a small breakup fee of two and a half billion dollars."

"That is a big chunk of change. Thank you, Susan."

* * *

It was Sunday night, and Daniel and Doris were lying in their bed. Daniel was reading the book given to him by Reverend Adams, and Doris was skimming through the day's newspapers, as she didn't get a chance to do so in the morning.

"It says here that the reverend dedicated this book to a Kathleen," Daniel said suddenly. "It says, 'See you sooner than later, always together.' Who is Kathleen?"

"You don't know?" Doris asked.

"Know what?"

"Kathleen's her daughter. She lost her when they were hit by a drunk driver. Kathleen was in grade school. I'm surprised she even mentioned her in the book," Doris informed.

"She never mentioned it to me, not even once," Daniel said quietly.

"Not surprising, knowing her," Doris remarked.

"Wouldn't that make people she works with respect her even more when they learn that she has gone through the same tragedy?" Daniel asked.

"She never talks about it because she feels it might get in the way of the therapies."

"I can understand that."

"She was a psychology professor when the accident happened. After going through grief counseling herself, she decided to become one too," Doris told Daniel.

"When was this?" he asked.

"It was before I started seeing her. She was going to theology school while working with me."

"She's quite an amazing individual."

"Yes, indeed. Do you know she is trying to build a grief and counseling center not far from the church?"

"I had no idea," Daniel said, truly astounded by the reverend's past.

CHAPTER 19
LAST CALL

THE NEXT MORNING, Daniel was in his office, sitting at his desk and sipping coffee from a large cup, when someone knocked at the door.

"Come on in!" he called out as he turned down the volume of the opera that was playing on his stereo.

Director of the Board Craig Barrett entered the office. He was in his early sixties and was dressed in a crisp gray suit.

"Hello, Daniel. Just wanted to say that Phil is a great choice to take over. I think there will be a unanimous vote by the board."

"Let the chips fall where they may," Daniel voiced slowly.

"I'm sorry," Craig uttered in an earnest whisper.

"I could not agree with you more."

"Will I be seeing you at lunch?" Craig asked as he turned around to leave.

"Yeah, I'll be there."

Craig nodded and left the office, allowing the door to quietly shut behind him.

Daniel brought his coffee mug closer to his lips and was about to take a sip when a sharp pain traveled down his left shoulder. The cup dropped from his hands and shattered, spilling coffee everywhere. He clutched his left shoulder, and his face twisted to form a grimace. He got out of his chair, trembling from the ache, and tried to find his medicine. However, it was no use. After a few seconds, he felt an agonizing throb in the middle of his chest. He realized that it was a heart attack.

He sat down again and reached for his phone, dialing his secretary's number. Laura picked up the phone immediately.

"Laura, you better call someone. I'm not doing so well," he managed to utter.

"Mr. Pallson, are you alright?" she asked, concern lacing her voice.

Daniel, however, could not reply, as he had collapsed over his desk, his hand still clutching his chest and his eyes open wide. When no response came from Daniel's end, Laura rushed into his office. As soon as she entered through the door and saw the slumped body of Daniel Pallson, she knew what had happened. She rushed to her desk and called 911, tears flowing from her eyes. After she had made the call, she once again hurried back into the office and helped Daniel lie on the floor.

"Hang in there, Mr. Pallson. The doctor is on his way." Daniel continued to writhe on the floor.

"You're gonna be fine," she said again.

After a few long minutes, Doctor Bird rushed into the office.

"What happened?" he asked.

"I don't know. He just collapsed," Laura told him.

Doctor Bird bent down in front of Daniel to check his condition. The faint sounds of an ambulance approaching could be heard through the open office doors before Daniel passed out.

* * *

Daniel was lying unconscious on the hospital bed, with Doris by his side, holding his hand. Dr. Walsh entered the room.

"Mrs. Pallson, I have the results of the tests. Do you have time to discuss them now?" he questioned.

"Sure, Doctor," Doris said.

Dr. Walsh led Doris to his office, and they both took their seats on the table opposite one another.

"I'm going to be honest with you, Mrs. Pallson, it doesn't look too good. It's a stroke related to the previous heart attack."

"Is there anything we can do?" she asked, a sliver of hope still alive in her hoarse voice.

"We can operate again, another surgery, but it will be risky. We cannot be sure of the results."

Doris didn't know how to respond to this. She felt completely broken and hollow from the inside—her soul drenched in sorrow and misery.

"We will need Daniel's permission to operate. We need to make a decision soon. There isn't a lot of time," the doctor told her before he got up and left Doris alone in the room.

Tears rolled down Doris's chin. She knew what this meant, that Daniel probably would not allow for another surgery. She knew that this might be the end. She cried for a long time before she mustered the courage to leave the doctor's office. Then she made her way back to Daniel's hospital room and took her place by his side.

After almost an hour had elapsed, he stirred.

"Darling, you're awake," she remarked, smiling for the first time in what seemed like a very long time.

Daniel slowly opened his eyes. There was a drastic difference between this stroke and the one he had in Iceland. His voice was weaker than it had ever been.

"Doris?" he whispered.

"I am here, darling. I am here."

He looked at his wife and noticed the tears rolling down her cheeks.

"Are you crying?" he asked.

"Oh, silly me," she said as she shook her head. Daniel raised a twitching hand and tried to wipe the tears off her face.

"You're not silly," he coughed. "Where am I?"

"At the hospital, you had another stoppage."

Doctor Walsh entered once again. Daniel looked up at him before asking, "Would you put down money on an old fart like me?"

"Depends how much." The doctor smiled.

"Are the odds in my favor?" Daniel questioned upfront.

"We can do the surgery…"

"But?"

"Your heart is in bad shape. There is no way to know the outcome. It could go either way."

A deafening silence rang in the room as Daniel paused to contemplate. However, instead of addressing the doctor, he turned toward Doris.

"I want to go home," he told her finally.

"You are home. We're in Boston," she said calmly.

"Iceland, I want to go home to Iceland."

Doris looked at the doctor then back at Daniel.

"Are you sure about this?" she asked.

"Never been sure of anything more in my life."

Reverend Adams's cell phone rang. The identification read, "Unidentified Caller." She answered it. "Hello." A voice was heard, but the connection was bad. "Who is this? We have a bad connection." The crackling from the bad connection continued. "What? Daniel, is this you? I'm having a hard time understanding you. You're going where? To see who? Thomas? Did you say Thomas? I lost you again. Hello?"

The reverend held the phone to her ear for a few seconds. "Daniel?" She then put the phone down on her desk and paused for a few seconds. She then dialed Daniel's number. The phone kept ringing, but she got a recording. She smiled in reflection as she put the phone back on her desk.

CHAPTER 20
THE BIGGEST DEAL OF ALL

Daniel's private jet pulled up on the tarmac. Jon, Anna, Magnus, his wife Erla, and Dagur awaited Daniel's arrival. Doris had pre-informed them about their return.

As the plane's engines winded down, the cabin door opened, and Doris walked down the stairs. She was greeted by Jon and the rest of the family. Two paramedics carefully helped Daniel down the stairs and strapped him into a wheelchair. Dr. Walsh also descended the airplane steps.

"Daniel, great to see you," Jon beamed.

Daniel, who rarely showed any emotion, stood up on quivering legs and gave his brother the biggest hug he had ever given anyone. Jon was pleasantly surprised.

"You got everything set up?" Daniel asked Jon.

"Yes, just like you asked," he replied.

"Are we gonna go fishing?" Dagur interjected from beside his father.

Jon nodded at him with a smile before pointing toward an SUV and a large rental van stationed a couple of hundred feet away.

"You have no idea how grateful I am to see all of you here. It means the world to me and Doris. Today is meant as a surprise for all of you. Please follow me along the way," Daniel told everyone.

Everyone voiced their approval in unison. Daniel entered the van with Doris, the doctor, and the paramedics while the rest of them seated themselves in the SUV. They drove away together from the airport.

The two vehicles made their way to a pristine valley owned by Daniel. The cars came to a halt outside a beautiful and splendid fishing lodge. Everyone stepped out on a bright and gorgeous Icelandic summer day.

Doris turned to Daniel. "So, this is the surprise? Is it finally open for lunch?" she asked.

"Lunch is only the beginning," Daniel told her.

As they were walking inside, the project manager of the fishing lodge arrived.

"Welcome all, please come inside!" he greeted.

After a few minutes of sauntering around the place, the entire family sat at a long table inside the lodge. Daniel, sitting at the head of the table, looked a bit frail but appeared to be in good spirits. He cleared his throat before speaking.

"A wise special someone recently said to me," he began and looked in Jon's direction with a smile before he continued, "that it is never too late to do something right. I didn't quite understand at the time, but now I do. So that is why we are here today. And, as you all know, I am not big on speeches, so…let's eat and go fishing!" He lifted his glass and clinked it with Jon's.

Everyone ate the tasty food and engaged in happy and cheerful conversations. Therein, Daniel finally felt at peace. He was content as he watched his family smiling, enjoying themselves, and having a good time.

After the family was full to the brim with the delicious meals they consumed, they made their way to the fishing dock. Jon helped seat Daniel in the back of the boat as a nurse carried his wheelchair. Doris, Anna, and Erla were keeping him company while Jon, Magnus, and Dagur were checking out the highest quality of fishing equipment money could buy already set up on the boat.

"How are you feeling?" Anna asked Daniel.

"Fine," he answered her and soon after started coughing uncontrollably. Doris leaned in to stroke his back and offered him a warm drink. He took a few small sips and recovered, but little drops of sweat could be seen on his forehead.

"Can we move the shade over?" Doris wondered, noticing Daniel's condition.

Erla stood up and drew the shades over Daniel, who assured the women that he felt fine.

The sun started to set after a few hours, but the three men were still out in the boat, trying to catch some fish. Jon stood next to Dagur, who was not doing well. He was frustrated and pounded the line on the water.

"It's not working!" he yelled.

"Patience, my boy, don't let it get to your head," Jon tried to get him to relax.

Suddenly, Magnus felt his fishing rod being pulled.

"I got one. I got one," he announced joyfully.

He started reeling it in as Daniel watched carefully from his seat on the boat. Magnus continued pulling it in. However, once again, the fish broke the line and swam away. Everyone was disappointed, and a few of them sighed.

A couple more hours elapsed, but Jon, Magnus, and Dagur were still failing miserably at catching any fish. It became clear to Daniel that they needed his help. So, with the help of Magnus, he knew it best if he, the master fisherman, took charge.

"Let me show you how it's done!" he exclaimed as he had Magnus set him up with the special setup made for disabled fishermen.

Everyone looked on with shock as Daniel was now in charge.

Dagur ran toward Daniel and handed him his fishing rod. The women looked on from their spots on the boat.

"It's time to get the big one," Daniel told them.

"There's no fish in the lake today," Dagur said sadly.

"Don't despair, my boy. Let me show you how it's done," Daniel repeated.

Daniel threw out the line with amazing grace. It was clear that he had done this many times before.

"Never hit the line on the water, my boy! Just let it slide over it," he instructed Dagur.

Daniel continued his attempts until he suddenly felt a pull on his fishing rod. He had caught a fish, and it was a big one.

"Come on, you can get it!" Dagur cheered him on.

"Is it the big one?" Magnus asked.

"Unbelievable," Daniel yelled. "I don't believe it! After all these years, he's back, but this time he's not gonna get away from us."

"Are you kidding, Uncle Dan? It's Godzilla!

"The one and only," says Daniel.

"They can live a long time. This son of a bitch has."

"Let out the line a bit, tire the fish right," Dagur remarked. When Daniel turned to look at him, he saw Thomas's face.

"You are right, boy," Daniel whispered as the salmon jumped over the surface of the river. Everyone looked at the enormous fish and gasped. However, Daniel paid them no attention. He was confusing his persistent dream with reality. His sole focus was his son's face.

"This time, we'll get it, Son!" he said to Dagur, still seeing and thinking it was Thomas.

"You are doing great, Dad. Keep the line tight," Thomas called.

The fish kept struggling, and Dagur came closer to aid him with the task. He grabbed the fishing net in order to help in landing the salmon, which jumped and wriggled. It was much closer.

"You can do it, Uncle!" Magnus whistled.

Jon also came closer to help. "It is huge," he commented.

"We did it, Dad! We did it! It's the one and only Godzilla!" Thomas cheered, as Daniel saw Thomas when he was twenty-four, shortly before he died.

Magnus marched ahead and pulled the huge salmon out of the water with Jon as all clapped and cheered. They clicked a number of pictures, and the air was thick with joy and glee. It was truly the dream fish that had gotten away twenty years ago.

"We did it, Son. We did it," Daniel mumbled, his eyes still set upon Thomas's face as they gave each other the best hug ever.

Dagur, so excited at the sight, ran toward Magnus and helped him release the giant fish into the river. For a few seconds, it did not move, which made everyone a bit anxious, as most fish left ever so quickly. Finally, Godzilla twitched a bit and softly swooshed away, which made everyone at ease.

When Jon turned to congratulate Daniel, his breath got caught in his chest. He saw that Daniel had a huge smile on his face, but his eyes were shut.

"Daniel, Daniel!" he shouted.

The nurse rushed over to check on Daniel, getting no response. Doris descended the boat and slowly made her way to Daniel's side. It was the longest walk of her life. Tears silently flowed down her face, even though she tried to stay composed for the sake of her family. Doctor Walsh came running and proceeded to check Daniel's pulse. He looked up at Doris's face and slowly, with a dreaded look on his face, shook his head, indicating that Daniel had passed away. And then there was complete silence. They all surrounded Daniel as most began to cry.

* * *

The sun was shimmering high in the sky, and the air had a special freshness to it. A beautiful yet sorrowful instrumental tune was playing while around a hundred people were gathered in order to attend Daniel's funeral. The burial took place in the Pallson family graveyard, where the graves went back up to six generations. Daniel was being buried beside his son, Thomas Pallson. There was a space left on the other side, allocated for Doris. Daniel's name had been engraved on an intricately carved gravestone. The music stopped, and Jon came forward to say a few words.

"Thank you all for coming! We will hopefully see you all in the house later. I don't have a lot to say, as I don't feel that my love for my brother, along with the void he left behind, can be put into words. So I'm simply going to announce his last wish. He wanted to transfer the property rights of the river valley to a trust overseen by his nephew, Magnus Pallson. He can use that money for the development of the land in whichever way he sees fit."

The attendees smiled at this announcement, and a few congratulated Magnus and shook his hand. Others headed back toward the main house. Doris, however, stayed behind. She stood by Daniel and Thomas's graves for a long time until the tears finally stopped flowing.

* * *

Reverend Adams was in her office, reading something on her computer. There was a sudden knock on the door, and Doris walked in. Reverend Adams stood up to greet her.

"Doris, my goodness. I am so glad to see you," she said as she threw her arms around Doris and gave her a warm hug.

"Good to see you too, and thank you for the flowers," Doris responded.

"It was the least I could do. How are you?"

"I'm fine, all things considered."

"I wish I could've gone with you to Iceland."

"It was a beautiful ceremony," Doris informed the reverend.

"That's good to hear. He deserved it. I just hope my time with Daniel helped him in some way."

"It most definitely did." Doris smiled as she handed the reverend an envelope. "Daniel wanted me to give this to you."

"What is it?" Reverend Adams asked.

"Please read it." Doris requested.

Reverend Adams tore open the envelope. Inside was a short, handwritten note and a small flash drive. She read the note.

"What might be the most fascinating thing of all is how much you've changed me. The Daniel who walked into your office and the one that came out are two different and distinct people altogether—a good dichotomy, huh?"

The reverend inserted the drive into the computer to look through its contents.

A picture popped up on her screen. The first picture showcased the whole family at the fishing lodge before they went to the river. Daniel had the biggest smile of them all. Adams clicked on the second picture. It was a beautiful sunset with Daniel being baptized by his brother in the shallow water of the lake shortly before he passed. The caption on the picture read, "Going to see Thomas."

All of a sudden, something else fell out of the envelope. It was a check made out to The Kathleen Adams Grief and Counseling Center for a staggering forty million dollars. It was a gift from Daniel. The memo line on the check read: "Best bet I ever lost! And for the record, you were right. The work we did was my biggest deal ever."

BOOMERANG

A POEM BY JENNIFER CURRAN

is it a personal journey?
this life this heart this soul
designed to illuminate God within
my thoughts, my pain circles around others
bringing the minotaur's curse to me

choice? Freedom?
Cruel to myself
A negation of who I am clouding my joy
The days pass by, years
The metamorphous a time lapse of unceasing
    procrastination

Is the reflection what is so painful?
Sometimes I amaze me with the lack of compassion within
The experiential need to empathize
As if thought weren't enough

But what is there?
The mystics draw me
Yet the stubbornness, the walls, the granite of my heart
    confuse me
Send me on a repetitious path
A human boomerang
Flipped by the hand of God
Turning head over heels endlessly till the centrifugal force
    hurls me
Back to my maker

NOTES

NOTES

NOTES

NOTES

NOTES

NOTES

NOTES

NOTES

NOTES

NOTES

www.ingramcontent.com/pod-product-compliance
Lightning Source LLC
LaVergne TN
LVHW061211290125
802363LV00037B/850